CASTLE CLODHA

May was visiting the little Scottish island of Clodha for the first time. She had fallen in love with the island of her ancestors; with its colourful history of witches, feuds, dark deeds and with its laird; Rory MacMhor, wild and strange, ruling like a feudal lord. But was this just a brief, romantic dream of happiness. Or could she make the dream come true?

CASTLE CLODHA

Castle Clodha

by

ALANNA KNIGHT

MAGNA PRINT BOOKS
Long Preston
North Yorkshire . England

British Library Cataloguing in Publication Data

Knight, Alanna
   Castle Clodha. – Large print ed.
   I. Title
   823'.914[F]   PR6061

   ISBN 0–86009–336–0

First Published in Great Britain 1972

Copyright © 1972 by Alanna Knight

Published in Large Print 1981 by arrangement with Anthony Sheil Associates Ltd. London

Printed and bound in Great Britain by
Redwood Burn Limited   Trowbridge

For Peggy and Roy Cramb

Chapter One

MY cases, ready packed, waited in the hall. I looked at my watch. Tomorrow at this time I would be in Scotland, heading for the Isle of Clodha off the west coast. Clodha and the grandmother I had never met. Tomorrow. It seemed a million miles away as my footsteps echoed hollowly through the empty rooms in that last-minute search for forgotten possessions.

This house where I was born was already a stranger. Once these rooms had held all the paraphernalia of my childhood: toys, prams, dolls. Once it had echoed with my parents' laughter, with the joys of a serene united family. Now all that was finished, that chapter in its existence ended. Even its echoes sounded strange, aloof, as if it prepared itself for the new tenants who would move in on Monday.

Monday. By then I would be settled on Clodha. I tried to imagine it: 'Clodha,' said the gazetteer, 'a small island with 200 inhabitants.' Would it be lonely, desolate? Was I being mad choosing such a place for a holiday?

'Yes, only two or three weeks. A holiday,' I told my friends.

'Make a month of it,' said our doctor. 'Get away somewhere new. You've earned a rest. A complete rest. You're far too pale.'

A complete rest. At twenty-three the idea seemed ridiculous. Yet it was only since the funeral I realised how exhausted I was, what a toll, physical and mental, Dad's illness had taken of me. Rushing home every evening from Sarah's boutique, shopping on the way, begrudging every hour I had to spend away from him, stubbornly refusing to let him spend his last months in hospital merely to die when there was no longer any hope. Together we treasured even a long miserable winter, pretending spring would bring health again. I could still see him sitting by the window, nodding in agreement, smiling wanly and looking down the street beyond the tiny garden he had loved but was no longer fit enough to cherish. . . . I could see that his eyes were already far away, listening for a call I could not hear.

Now the garden too was empty of colour, the last of the daffodils had withered on his grave. This was the sad season he had never liked, neither spring nor summer, when the yellows and mauves had all faded and it was too soon for the flamboyant reds and blues of summer.

I closed my eyes listening to the sounds of the street. Children played, dogs barked, birds twittered, the No. 26 bus braked to a stop. These sounds had been my first memories. Now they were familiar but comforting no longer, part of a past from which I was irrevocably severed.

And suddenly it came to me, standing alone in an empty room with a chill spring wind echoing down the silent chimney. The sound of the sea, a rough wild sea. I was falling, drowning ... An indescribable crawling sense of horror, of evil and danger. I wanted to turn and run, open the front door, run from tomorrow ...

The bell pealed and there was Sarah.

'May? Are you all right? May, what's the matter?' And in a sudden rush of sympathy she put her arm around me.

11

'There, there – this must be awful for you. Look, I've come to see you to the airport.'

'No, Sarah. Not on a Saturday. What about the boutique?'

'Hang the boutique. Dilys might as well learn. She'll need to take on some responsibility while you're away.' She sighed, looking at the curtainless windows, and, sad-eyed, tapped her foot on the floorboards. 'Gives you the creeps, doesn't it?'

Relief flooded through me, warm and comforting. So it wasn't merely my imagination. The sense of horror came from the empty house, the desolate echoes of deserted rooms. Sarah felt it too.

'Come along, May dear. Everything will be different when you come back and stay in our flat. Mum's looking forward to having you. It'll be just like having another girl in the family, she says. . . .'

I smiled and said yes, listening to her plans and thought of the small pleasant home, overcrowded already with two sisters and a brother younger than Sarah.

No, it wasn't only leaving this house to live in new surroundings that gave me the horrors. The awareness of a rough sea,

12

that momentary sense of drowning, had something to do with Clodha.

'Cheer up, May.'

I shook myself, smiled wanly. I couldn't tell her, and picking up my cases I walked out of the house without a single backward glance. Some neighbours who had been good and kind always, and there from the beginnings of my remembered life, kissed me goodbye, wished me well. 'Goodbye, goodbye' – a wave, here and there eyes bright with unshed tears, then the street was gone and we were speeding along the motorway. Listening to Sarah talk, a glazed smile on my face and a growing numbed conviction in my heart told me I would never return to this London suburb. No flat with Sarah and her kind mum. No more boutique. Such things were past, finished. Not that I wasn't grateful or didn't want them. I did. I longed for the safe security of warm familiar places and people.

Only I knew I couldn't have them. Some dark inevitable tide had reached out and claimed me, severing all hope of returning to the life I had known. Even my friend Sarah, these streets, these beloved landmarks I had known all my life, were remote and unreal, like scenes vaguely recalled from an old film seen long ago.

'You are lucky,' said Sarah as we waited in the departure lounge for the Glasgow plane. 'I love an early holiday. Wish I was coming with you, but it's the worst possible time to leave the shop with the new fashions and the spring collection in everyone's mind.' She sighed and looked anxiously into my face. 'You will be all right, won't you?' I smiled, of course. 'That's better. Clodha will be heavenly – I bet you won't want to come back to grimy old London.'

'Perhaps I won't be able to come back, Sarah.' And the words were out as if someone else had spoken.

Sarah frowned. 'What on earth do you mean, May? Of course you're coming back. What about the boutique – all our plans ...?'

'Attention, attention. Will passengers for the B.406 flight to Glasgow please join the plane. Please have your boarding cards ready ...'

Then Sarah was gone, a slim elegant figure, unreal as a model from *Vogue*, waving goodbye, goodbye. Happy holiday.

Less than two hours later I was in Scotland and by lunchtime in a train heading for Oban. Spring had come to the world again in a froth of white blossom, of pale green trees, of shaggy Highland beasts glowering in fields and gentle lambs skipping. Castles, ruined and noble, cars and buses on the roads, all rushed past against an eternal background of distant blue hills, like a ribbon of film going too fast, slotted here and there with the sparkling ribbon of a shining tree-lined river. Sometimes I caught sight of my own reflection in the window, lips parted, eyes glowing, smiling. Long straight hair, so dark red it looked black. Wide-set blue eyes and the high cheekbones of my Highland father and his race. A London girl born and bred, I shared other stranger things with these unknown island ancestors.

I shivered, afraid to remember them. An inbuilt radar for disaster and danger. Danger was so tangible, I could almost smell it. There were vivid strange dreams too, more than ordinary dreams, more a

15

consciousness of other worlds that existed besides this one of sight and sound and being.

I never told anyone for fear of being laughed at. Even gentle Sarah, kind but prosaic, could not conceal her mockery, her scepticism. 'All nerves and nonsense. This e.s.p. business is sheer imagination, a fashionable gimmick.'

Only my father understood, because I had inherited the Sight from him. His own death was no surprise and he viewed it, prepared for it, philosophically.

'Never run against the tide of life, May lass, you can't fight destiny.' For a moment through that sunlit window I could hear his voice, see him smiling across the gulf that divided us for the span of my mortal years. I opened my eyes as though I had received a benediction and the terrible oppression had gone.

I was on holiday, off to an adventure in a strange land. I was young and healthy and I had faith in destiny's hand.

I sighed with pleasure. It was so long since I had been away from London even for a day. Since Dad's illness, Sarah had done the extra fashion buying, the shows.

16

And somehow I had dropped out of the happy crowd of extroverts we called our friends. Boys came and went, but I could never get even mildly interested with a life that left neither time nor desire for shared devotion. Dad must have my every moment for the little time that remained. Last summer he was already too ill for me to leave him. Two summers ago Sarah and I took her car and motored to the west coast of Scotland for the first time. Up the long twisting coast of Wales, magic with memories of Merlin and King Arthur, then the pastoral beauty of the English Lake District and so into Galloway and the rugged west coast of Scotland.

The weather had been superb until we crossed over the Border and then, glowering on us, it rained almost every day. Still there was one day of fretful sunshine on Loch Maree and magical glimpses of majestic mountains, shy deer, pine woods and dark castles, sombre and ruined. This wild land held beauty and awesome enchantment and it was mine. It called to something deep inside me, a call clearly heard and answered. Rain and all, I loved every moment and hated Sarah for grumbling.

Dad had laughed when I told him. 'That's because you're part Highland. The elements that are natural to your own country will never bother you, my lass. You'll always feel the same deep-down loyalty a true Scot feels for his own homeland. Aye, no matter how many continents, how many miles, divide you from it.'

He had sighed, looking at a gold-framed oil painting of a Highland scene, painter unknown, which hung above the mantelpiece, a birthday present from a junk shop with my first cheque from Sarah's boutique. Poverty had driven him as a young man into exile from Clodha. Full of the hopes, dreams, the unfailing optimism of the true romantic, he regarded London as the mecca in which no able-bodied honest man could ever starve. Disillusioned, he found that cities and towns had their own kinds of bitter poverty and after many adversities he took a job with the local council and, prosperous for once, met and married Mother, daughter of Lowland Scots from Angus who had been uprooted by the Second World War.

The council provided them with a house and there I was born. For many years we were happy together, then Mother, in hospital for what she believed was a routine operation, strangely died. I was seventeen, in my first term at the School of Design and Dressmaking, and when the shock abated I grew up very quickly, looking after Dad.

Two years ago Sarah's aunt left her a legacy. With it and my designs the boutique was born. Life thereafter was uneventful, often a little dull, for love never came my way as the books and magazines glowingly promised. None of the men I had met thus far ever really touched my heart. Love, I thought, was not for me. . . .

I shared the passenger deck of the Oban ferry (twice per day to Clodha) with a shepherd, a huge flock of sheep and a sad-faced man in a bowler hat. Hoping I would get another chance to explore the mainland, I watched it vanish in a kind of bleak despair, as I considered what reception awaited me on Clodha.

My grandmother had paid little attention through the years to her son and

19

his fortunes, even less to her granddaughter. Dad had left a letter to be sent after his death, which I could only presume contained some plea to look after me, because she replied very promptly, saying she was sorry and of course I would be welcome at any time. As if in afterthought, she added a postscript saying that Clodha was at its best in early summer, perhaps I would like to come immediately.

A ragged smudge of dark blue appeared on the horizon. When I asked the shepherd, who was eyeing my suitcases with polite curiosity, if this was Clodha he smiled and shook his head.

'No, no. What you are seeing is Eilean na Gealach.' We drew closer and the smudge was like a dark hand reaching out of the sea.

'Does anyone live there?'

'Ach no. Only the birds and wild things. The Atlantic currents are fierce between Gealach and Clodha.' He looked at me, smiling. 'And would Clodha be your destination?' When I said yes, he nodded. 'Then the winds are blowing for you. A week back and you would have been sitting it out in Oban waiting for the wild seas to die. Just a wee touch of a storm from Gealach and the ferry cannot get across. Is that not so, Andrew?'

The man in the bowler had nodded sadly in the direction of my luggage. 'Clodha's not very fine for tourists, I'm thinking. They have not the television or the cinema and the dancing only sometimes.'

'Ach well,' said the shepherd, searching my face for signs of dismay at this announcement, 'it is none the worse for that, Andrew. Not the place for a young lady on her own, though . . .'

'My grandmother, Mrs. Lachlan, lives there.'

'So you're kin to the Lachlans. You will be all right then,' he added with evident relief. Then, eyes twinkling, he said: 'I would not have wished a nice-like young lady as yourself to be going alone among the wild MacMhors.'

I didn't get a chance to find out the intriguing answer to that one, as the pilot leaned out of his window shouting for Andrew and both men hurried away. It didn't matter, I had other things than the wild MacMhors, whoever they might be, to

21

interest me.

The ferry was passing Eilean na Gealach, great rocks like the fingers of some grotesque giant hand thrusting their way out of the sea. And although the waters around us were silken-smooth, pretty as grey taffeta, between the rocks of the island a huge sea boiled and moaned, hurling the edge of its fury across the stretch of water that separated it from Clodha. Clodha – I looked across eagerly to where it rested peacefully uneventfully green on the blue sea. There was a white harbour, a cluster of houses and ribbon of road twisting up the steep cliff-face. On the hill-top, dominating the scene, a dark castle straight from the pages of a Jacobite romance.

Five minutes later we were alongside. Down went the ramp, and like a benediction out came the sun. A welcome, I thought, until I noticed that far above our heads Castle Clodha waited, beneath the grim shadow of the only cloud remaining in the sky.

Chapter Two

'MAY. May Lachlan?' I turned round and a pretty girl with long black hair climbed out of an estate car.

'Hello. I'm Katrine Lachlan. We're cousins of a kind,' she added with a smile. 'Jump in.' She pushed my cases into the back of the car which held feathery evidence as well as the smell of hens.

'Gran's looking forward to having you. She's getting old, of course, and she only has me now. I stay with her and look after the hens. Did you have a good journey? Hungry?'

All these remarks were thrown off in a staccato speed very much in keeping with her driving, and accompanied by a lot of horn as she drove a path among the sheep baaing on the cluttered quayside.

A chicken farm with an ageing grandmother seemed quite the wrong setting for a girl as attractive and young as Katrine Lachlan, especially when she slowed down at a petrol station and a young man rushed out to greet her. By the look in his eye, he obviously found her attractive too. Not that I understood a word they said to each other, but, Gaelic or no, I knew flirtation when I saw it. They were so taken with each other she almost forgot to introduce me.

'My cousin May. Meet Colin MacMhor.'

As he took my hand, I noticed he also had black hair, a rather long nose and light-coloured eyes. His appearance left a vague feeling of disappointment, somehow he had narrowly missed being very handsome.

Our hands had barely met before the car whizzed away with a final wave from Katrine and an insolent toot on the horn.

'Are we really cousins?' I asked.

'Only by marriage. Your Uncle Donald married my mother when she was a widow and I was four. That's a long time ago,' she sighed. 'I'm nearly twenty-seven. And on the shelf too,' she added cheerfully, 'according to Gran.'

Remembering the pleasant flirtation with Colin MacMhor I had witnessed, I said: 'I don't think she need have many fears.'

'Really?' She looked pleased and took a hairpin bend with skill and an alarming lack of brakes. 'Colin – back there – has been asking me to marry him for years, but I can't decide somehow.' She frowned. 'They're an unlucky family, the MacMhors.'

'The wild MacMhors?'

She laughed. 'News certainly gets around. Old scandals too. I suppose your father told you their shocking history.'

He hadn't, but I nodded vaguely, eager to hear more. 'You said they were unlucky?'

'Oh yes, ever since the eighteenth century when the chieftain who was fond of the ladies had the ill-luck to seduce a witch. Eventually he got tired of her and starved her to death by locking her in the castle and leaving her to die. So she cursed the lot of them. I know it sounds ridiculous, but it lingers on somehow. They can never escape disaster.'

And staring at the sinister pile that was Castle Clodha I believed her. I had a strange feeling that on this island anything could happen and – probably did. There was something here that suggested other laws than the natural ones, other worlds hidden in the dark heather and the wild seas at Gealach.

Katrine stopped outside a small cottage. Like others we had passed on the road, it was whitewashed, sparkling with paint, the windows gleaming.

'Here we are.'

I followed her inside and after a lifetime spent with modern furniture I was delighted at the prospect before us. An old loom, a settle, an oak table, rocking-chairs, hand-made rugs, a stone fireplace with a bright fire gleaming. All spelt romance to my city girl's heart, so did the lovely fragrance everywhere. I sniffed the air and Katrine smiled.

'That's peat. There's no coal here on the island. Come and see the rest.' She opened the door into a kitchen and through it a modern bathroom. 'These were added quite recently,' she said proudly. 'At one time all cooking was done at the fire in the living-room and Gran still hates these new-fangled electric cookers, and as for washing machines, well, that's too revolutionary to be decent.' She chuckled, pointing to a large hip-bath which stood in one corner. *That* was all the bathroom she had as a bride, a hip-bath taken out once a week in front of the fire. However, even Gran appreciates her nice bathroom, carrying buckets of water was never a joke, especially in winter.'

I followed her up a narrow wooden stair. 'This used to be a ladder in my childhood, the bedrooms up here were just a loft.' She held up a finger to her lips as we passed the first door. 'Ssh, Gran will be having her afternoon nap,' and she opened the door opposite. 'Hope you don't mind sharing with me. You can have the big bed, at least it has a modern mattress – and I'll have the one by the window.' And glowering down through the window at us was Castle Clodha, home of the Clan MacMhor, the wild and unlucky MacMhors. I could almost hear Sarah's practical voice dismissing it as: 'Rubbish and coincidences, of course.'

I wondered. 'The only view I've ever had from a window was another house exactly the same on the other side of the street. How lovely to have a ruined castle.'

Katrine paused in heaving covers off the bed. 'It may need a few repairs here and there, but ruined it certainly is not. You're looking on the proud home of Roderick

Malcolm MacMhor, chief of the Clan MacMhor,' she added proudly, 'and every bit of the land you see from here belongs to him. He's Colin's cousin — they're all related — but he and Colin don't get along.' There was a loud knock from downstairs. 'That'll be Andrew for his eggs. And I haven't even sorted them. Can you manage?'

She rushed downstairs and as I unpacked I decided that the inhabitants of Clodha were as sensitive about social prestige as any county lady. I looked up at Castle Clodha. It looked completely deserted and was large enough to make heating a distinct trial. Its situation suggested that a winter spent in it would be almost suicidal too.

Thrusting my emptied suitcases out of sight, I decided I was certainly on the threshold of an unusual holiday. Wild MacMhors, a witch who had cursed them, besides undoubted family feuds. And a splendidly romantic though somewhat creepy-looking castle perched on a hill. I imagined Roderick, chief of the MacMhors, angrily pacing its hall, an ageing patriarch clad in tartan, with flowing white hair like an Old Testament prophet.

I put my nose out of the bedroom door and suddenly at the smell of frying bacon discovered I was very hungry. Katrine had dealt with the egg situation and was preparing a meal for us both. After I had tucked away my third slice of home-baked bread (and raspberry jam prepared from fruit bushes beyond the kitchen window), I was despatching the last crumbs when my grandmother came down stairs. Katrine sprang to her feet and I followed suit. She gave me a tiny bird-like hand, a frail old woman with a small face and vivid blue eyes, framed by white hair, who at first glance bore little resemblance to my father. Her appearance suggested gentleness, but this was not the case.

'*Is e do bheatha,*' she said, and when I stammered 'Hello' she was obviously disappointed. She addressed Katrine in the same language and Katrine rushed to pull out a chair for her and there was a sharp interchange in Gaelic between them.

'You are welcome, Grand-daughter. Katrine is telling me you have not the Gaelic. I had thought any son of my house would have given to his daughter his own tongue to speak,' she said bitterly. 'Please sit down,' she added, indicating the chair at her side.

I sat there with a polite smile, chilled inside by her cold impersonal greeting. I wanted her to kiss me, to start talking about Dad. She did neither. So tiny, so indifferent, yet as I watched there was something of Dad in her face and suddenly I began to cry.

Almost absently, she leaned over, patted my hand. 'There, there, child. Do not be crying.' She added some words in the Gaelic, but there was no warmth in them, nor in the hand she withdrew hurriedly as though physical contact embarrassed her.

In that too she was like my father. One of those people whose emotions are under constant control, who find it hard to 'give' love. A man of few words, it cost Dad agonies to show his affection, and after Mother died how I missed her hugs and kisses, her easy demonstrativeness. But as the years passed I never had reason to doubt that my father truly loved me, his actions showed he did more plainly than any words. And suddenly at this stiff old woman's side I guessed how much she had loved her younger son, who had broken her heart – and her pride – when he left Clodha never to return.

The conversation limped along between us and I was glad of Katrine's presence. I learned that there was no public transport on the island, but Katrine, laughing at the dismay on my face, said:

'There's an old bike in the toolshed. I used it before I got the car. Have it any time you feel like exploring.'

'Why don't you show it to her, Katrine,' said Grandmother, who had been showing her disinterest in the talk between us by yawning delicately and closing her eyes. As we took our leave, she said something in Gaelic and once outside Katrine looked rather uncomfortable.

'I hope you won't feel offended, May. Grandmother says she hopes you will lengthen your skirts a little for the time you are on Clodha. Yes, I know it is the fashion, but Gran feels decency is more important.'

After inspecting the bicycle Katrine went off to feed the hens and, glad of an excuse to be on my own, I went to the bedroom and wrote a promised letter to Sarah: 'You'll be glad to know I arrived safely and Clodha is beautiful ...' But I didn't tell her of my mixed feelings, the tumult of emotions Clodha was arousing in me or of my grandmother's cold reception.

'Take the bike down to the post,' Katrine had said. 'No one will mind where you go, or what short cuts you take, as long as you remember to close their gates.'

The bike was rusted and old and as I blew up the tyres they wheezed alarmingly, so that I suspected a slow puncture. Perhaps it would carry me to the harbour and back. Nevertheless, as my last dealings had been with a junior cycle, aged thirteen, I mounted it with some anxiety. Miraculously I stayed on and set an uncertain course downhill to the general store-cum-post office.

Once away from the cottage, I was overcome with curiosity and a small desire to return to an unequal struggle for conversation with Gran. I could hardly expect Katrine to entertain me, so I took the hint and explored, starting up the cliff road I had noticed from the ferry, which led to Castle Clodha. There was a stiff wind blowing in my face, so I pushed the bike, enjoying the scenery with the virtuous feeling that toil made it somehow more worth while. Far below the steep cliff-face on a glassy sea the mist gathered, already creeping over the harbour and across the wild heather behind the houses. Here and there the blue of bell heather intermingled with the searing yellow flame of gorse. Far above my head, sea birds, white and unrecognisable, sent their echoing cries across the sea, and as they saw some fishing boat returning to harbour they hovered smoothly towards it, screaming hunger and excitement.

The scene before me was pretty and peaceful as a picture postcard. I couldn't imagine this little world shattered by storms, or severed by man's lust for vengeance.

Suddenly the road vanished in a huddle of crofts and over a high stone wall a mere tantalising glimpse of what must be the back of Castle Clodha. A cart-track led through a gate, across to a stone byre from which emerged the restless sounds of cattle and the rich smells of pig manure.

Remembering Katrine's instructions about gates, I found myself on the other side of the wall where two stone cottages stood roofless and derelict and the track I followed ended with a small gate leading into a spinney of trees. I was close to Castle Clodha at last: A forbidding tall mass of grey stone and, high over my head, a pepperpot turret with one window, barred.

Aware that I was now undoubtedly trespassing, but determined to satisfy my curiosity, having come this far, I pushed the bicycle along the path, wondering if I had enough nerve to continue on through the spinney for a closer look at the front of the castle.

Suddenly I stopped in my tracks. An odd prickling sensation on the back of my neck said I was being watched. From the barred window a pale face stared down at me. A girl with long red-gold hair. Beautiful, I thought, even at this distance.

Her lips were moving. She was trying to tell me something. I put my hand up to shield my eyes for a better look at the window, and as I did so, a new sound shattered the sunlit afternoon. A sheep bleating in terror, somewhere close at hand, inside the spinney.

Opening the gate, I looked back at the castle window, but the girl had gone. The unseen sheep was now screaming blue murder, so I followed the noise rapidly and found a new lamb on still-tottery legs. Somehow it had crawled under the barbed wire which enclosed the spinney away from the sheep's attention and, struggling to escape, it had got it its wool firmly entangled on the barbs.

Kneeling down, I took a firm grip on the struggling animal and managed to release him strand by strand, while his mother, watching us from a cautious distance on the other side of the wire, kept up a pathetic chorus to her offspring's bleating. I discovered that restoring them to each other was easier said than done, for the wire enclosure was too high to drop him over on to the other side without injury. As I tried to manoeuvre him underneath the wire, he wriggled out of my hands and skipped off in terror, back into the spinney, taking refuge in the protection of the shrubbery.

A ridiculous and quite inadequate Bo-peep, I crawled about on hands and knees trying to winkle him out. At last I had him cornered, the din of terrified sheep, alarmed by his cries, like all hell let loose.

Tucking him firmly under my arm, I emerged from the gate. Carefully closing it behind me, I glanced at the castle window and felt rather aggrieved that there was no longer any witness to my rescue operation. Had she been telling me about the lamb whose struggles would be obvious from that barred window? Or, I wondered with a pang of unease, had she merely been warning me that I was on private ground?

Too late I realised the latter surmise had been the right one. I stopped, frozen in my tracks, as a big black collie with bared yellow teeth hurtled towards me out of nowhere. I staggered back against the fence, holding up the lamb well above my head, away from those snapping teeth. Growling, it dragged at my skirt and utterly terrified I shouted, quite ineffectually: 'Home. Go home. Good dog – go home.'

Ignoring my pleas, the dog kept its hold on my skirt. Desperately I looked around for help. Even the sheep had sense enough to retire and appease their curiosity at the outcome of the affray by huddling together at a safe distance.

The whole world seemed deserted. What on earth would I do now?

Chapter Three

I HEARD a faint whistle, a human one. The dog pricked up his ears, let go my skirt, but still growling lay down at my feet. There was no mistaking the 'on guard' position – as I soon discovered when a sharp snap of teeth in the direction of my ankles counteracted my stealthy edging towards the shelter of the spinney.

'Oh, do go away. Nice dog. *Go home.*'

The whistle was shriller now and from the side of the castle appeared the figure of a man.

'Call off your dog, will you,' I shouted, but the man ignored me, strolling towards the scene in an insolently unhurried fashion.

'Would you *mind* calling him off?' I

shouted again, trying to sound pleasant and adding a nervous smile, as if I wasn't terrified out of my wits and this sort of thing happened regularly.

He had almost reached us. A tall, slim young man, in worn tweed jacket and a somewhat faded kilt.

'Would you mind ...?' I asked again. Although the situation was perfectly obvious to anyone, he still didn't speak and I realised I might be in a pretty fix explaining my presence on private ground if he 'had only the Gaelic', as Katrine had described the condition of half the island's population.

Nearness brought a tanned face with high cheekbones and the kind of dead straight black hair that would be forever falling into his eyes. Eyes that were a colour I remembered – from somewhere. Yes, I had it, the amber glow of sunset on Loch Maree after a storm. They were beautiful eyes, wide-set, luminous, and he might well have been handsome but for the angry set of black brows and the steely expression of a mouth that didn't look at if smiling was its normal occupation.

Still clutching my bleating lamb well out

of range, I said slowly and patiently, nodding towards the dog:

'Please—call—him—off.'

He snapped his fingers and the dog leaped to his side. I didn't take immediate advantage of my release, for both man and dog glared ferociously, as if they would have enjoyed rending me to shreds.

'And where the devil do you imagine you're taking that lamb?' the man asked softly. So he could speak English and, ignoring the dangerous note in his voice, suddenly my Lachlan temper was broken.

'It's rather obvious, don't you think?' He watched me stonily. 'All right. I'm stealing it,' I said furiously. 'Yes, there's my bicycle over there. I was just tucking the silly creature under my arm to ride down to the village. And sell it, of course.' With great dignity, that I certainly wasn't feeling at that moment, I added: 'Now, if you could possibly control your dog, I'll complete what I've been trying patiently to accomplish for the past ten minutes.' Gently I put the lamb on the ground and it didn't need an added 'shoo' from me to rush across the pasture to where its mother, bolder than her huddled companions, left their ranks to welcome the prodigal's return with a great many nosings and baa-ings.

'Instead of turning your dog on people, you'd be better training him to keep the sheep and their lambs together ...'

'May I remind you that you're on private property?' the man interrupted sharply, obviously in no mood to appreciate a list of his misdemeanours.

'You needn't worry,' and carefully dusting evidence of dog's paws from my skirt — its teeth, strangely, had left no impression — 'I have no intentions of lingering.'

'May I ask you where you came by *that?*' he said, following me to where the bicycle lay.

'You can. But I don't see that it is any of your business.'

'Only that when last I saw it, it happened to be the property of a Miss Katrine Lachlan.'

'It still is,' I said sweetly. 'Didn't I tell you? This is my day in the year for crime. I thought I would have a ball, wander on to private property, steal a lamb — having, of course, taken the precaution of bringing a

40

stolen bike to help carry away any other stolen goods I happened to come across.'

He didn't look at all amused, so I added in exasperation: 'For your information, Miss Katrine Lachlan happens to be my cousin. She also just happens to be the very good friend of your master' – I nodded towards Castle Clodha – 'who is, I believe' – and I said it very slowly relishing his discomfort – 'the chief of the MacMhors.'

'Indeed,' he said, faint amusement on his face where there should have been embarrassment.

'Indeed,' I said. I'd show him that switch to charm was too late, I thought, ignoring the smile that completely transformed his stern face. 'And when you tell your mistress . . .'

'My – *what?*'

'Your mistress, the MacMhor's lady, or whatever she is called. Oh, for goodness' sake, you know who I mean. She was up there. There,' and I pointed to the barred window in the turret. He swung round, following the direction of my hand with the strangest expression. Startled? No – more than that, he looked actually scared. For the first time I felt rather sorry for him.

Perhaps he was in for a terrible row. Perhaps, despite that pretty young face and the lovely red-gold hair, she was an absolute dragon.

'Yes,' I said calmly, wishing the interview was over, and I on my way. 'She saw the whole thing, she watched me rescue the lamb.' He continued to stare at the window, frowning, bewildered. 'If you want a character reference, ask her,' I added wearily. 'Now, may I go please?'

'Stealing bicycles and lambs and wandering on private property . . . Yes, I'm thinking it is a character reference you'll be needing, right enough.' He was trying hard, but the effort to concentrate on anything but that barred window was so considerable that almost with pity I wondered if he was in love with her. 'Before you leave is there any other crime you would like to confess to?' he added with a smile that lifted the corners of those strange amber eyes.

But my sense of humour was strangely evaporated, I was in no mood for somewhat hearty teasing. 'No,' I said, and grabbing the bicycle swung myself into the saddle. Unfortunately I accomplished this with more speed than grace and ruined a dignified exit as bicycle and I collapsed in an untidy heap, with a yell from me, at his feet.

'Er, not hurt, are you?' he said offering his hand, unable to restrain his mirth. I was furious, longing to slap that smiling face.

'I'll manage, thank you. And you can tell your master the MacMhor,' I yelled at him, 'that I called and tell him also that I think his factor is the most thoroughly rude, disagreeable, ungracious man I have ever met.'

With slow measured tread he seized the handlebars. He was quite unsmiling now. I remembered too that slow lilting yet somehow dangerous voice and an instinct for disaster told me it would be madness to provoke this man. He was so close all the golden colour had left his eyes. In rage they were black, lustreless as obsidians, menacing as storm-clouds over a Highland loch.

Yet he smiled and bowed slightly. 'I will give him your message. Yes, I think your opinion of me will amuse him. It will amuse him very much.'

Furiously I cycled away, wobbling

down the path between the derelict crofts and so on to the cliff road. It was there I noticed the puncture. He must have seen it and enjoyed a good laugh that my disasters for the day weren't yet over. Now I would have to push the wretched object all the way back to Gran's.

And as if I hadn't had my share of trials and tribulations for one day the rain began, a steady drizzle, growing heavier each minute. I was in for a thorough soaking to cool down my temper. I trudged miserably along the road, the harbour far below now hidden by mist and rain and Gran's cottage still far away. My sweater and its matching skirt, kingfisher blue, new and so elegant, before their encounter with lamby hoofs and doggy paws, were soon drenched and bedraggled.

I stopped, wondering where I could find shelter and, as if on cue, a pale face stared out of the door of one of the isolated cottages. A little girl. She beckoned me inside and for a moment I was certain the child who stood there was a wraith, a ghost. She was tiny, her hair silver-white and long, white too her face and her eyes a pale gold. I followed her eagerly enough, expecting her mother to appear. But, once inside, she closed the door and I was in for another shock. As she turned, I noticed that her body, although tiny, was a woman's, and knew that curious agelessness belonged to one who would never be more than a child in mind.

Considering the broken ancient sticks of furniture, Gran's cottage seemed opulent by comparison. Then, as my eyes grew accustomed to the dimness, I saw other pale faces in the room, looking over my shoulder, motionless, disembodied.

I stepped back in horror to find the faces belonged on an old worn tapestry which completely covered one wall. I saw the skeins of silks too and some sections bright with new thread. The sharp blue and white of the St. Andrew's cross. Then a face too, which I recognised. The red-gold hair of the lady of MacMhor.

The girl gathered her box of silks and retired to a chair opposite me.

'What a beautiful tapestry,' I said, and took a closer look, 'it must be very hard work repairing it,' and I thought, You'd need good eyes too, especially in this light. When she didn't answer, I looked out of the window. 'The rain's very heavy,' I said politely, 'Will it last long?'

But the girl in the chair seemed to have forgotten me. Hugging her silks, eyes closed, she began to sing softly, swaying to and fro. I listened smiling, interested. Suddenly she stopped. Her eyes opened and she pointed to me, saying something in Gaelic, but she didn't address me, she was talking over my shoulder to the people in the tapestry.

I was thoroughly alarmed. Gaelic is a very expressive language and the impact of those unknown words lent a drama and urgency to one phrase which she repeated over and over . . .

Suddenly it was as if the cloud had lifted. With a gentle smile she stood up, offered me her chair. But alas, such signs of hospitality were too late. Rain or no rain, I could stay no longer in this weird cottage where there was little to choose between the flesh-and-blood face before me and the others in the tapestry, for all bore a strong resemblance, the same slight smile, the same look of somehow fixed intent.

I said I really must go and thanked her politely. At the gate I turned and saw her making the sign against all evil, the Sign of the Cross. Then without another look the door was hurriedly closed.

My knees were shaking as I trundled the bicycle down the wet road. What on earth had ever given me that fleeting idea that Clodha was beautiful? In the rain it was bleak, miserable, with all those lovely colours swept away by heavy mist.

What had Sarah said? 'Go. It will cheer you up.' Was that only yesterday? It seemed a million years ago. Cheer me up indeed. I wished she could see me now, a sorrier sight than on any of my London days. I supposed that Sarah imagined a peaceful setting where nothing ever happened more exciting than a stray cow, or a marooned lamb. Yet in the few hours I had been on Clodha more had happened to me than in months of the busy hurly-burly of commuting from the suburbs to Sarah's boutique in Chelsea.

I had provoked a tongue-tied disapproving attitude in my chilly unwelcoming grandmother. For my solitary good deed with the lamb I had probably ruined my new sweater and skirt, had been accused of trespassing by an

47

uncouth young man and narrowly escaped being savaged by his dog. My only walking shoes squelched water at every step and were probably beyond means of restoration. In addition, I had a strange idea that I had been cursed in Gaelic by the weird woman in the cottage, who was in all probability the witch of Clodha.

If all this could happen in a few hours I could reasonably expect a memorable three weeks.

An elderly Ford car tooted on the road behind me. I made room for it respectfully, with some hopes of a lift. The window reeled down and the face of the MacMhor factor stared out at me:

'Got a puncture, I see.' He noted that, I felt, with unnecessary relish. 'Jump in and I'll give you a lift to the village.' He smiled as he said it and I had to admit looked more than slightly human, in fact, I grudgingly admitted to myself, very attractive at that moment. But my hurt pride won out against charming overtures. He had been jolly rude and I jolly well wouldn't accept *his* charity.

I shook my head. 'No thank you,' I said coldly. 'I enjoy walking in the rain.'

'Not pushing a bicycle, surely?'

'But of course.'

'At least let me put it in the car for you. Look, there's plenty of room in the back.'

For a moment I was tempted. 'Come on,' he said, with a grin, 'it will only make me an accessory to the Crime of the Stolen Bicycle.'

I could see him returning it, having a good laugh with Katrine at my expense, see them both shaking their heads sadly over the strange ways of foreigners. At that moment I felt militantly English as I had never done before. 'I'll manage, thank you.'

'Be it as you wish.' He closed the window and went off down the road without a backward glance, leaving me to 'enjoy' my walk in the rain. I was furious with myself, feeling that I had also lost round two.

At Gran's cottage I peeled off my wet garments to the accompaniment of Katrine's amused glances:

'May, what a mess. See here and I'll dry them. Why on earth didn't you take a raincoat?'

'Because it looked such a lovely day,' I

protested, tired of being made feel a fool yet again.

She gave me a pitying look. 'You must never rely on the weather here. It can change so quickly. Look, I have to rush off now. There's hot water for a bath.' At the door she paused. 'Gran's back in bed, she'll be awake but resting. She only comes downstairs for a while in the afternoons. Doctor's orders, since she had pleurisy a couple of months ago.'

Perhaps I had misjudged her, and weakness, illness, had accounted for her lack of enthusiastic welcome for the grand-daughter she had never seen, I thought, as I bathed and changed. Upstairs I found her sitting up in bed reading an enormous family Bible. As the print was small, the light poor, I concluded that life on Clodha must be kinder to eyesight than it was in towns, as there was no evidence of spectacles. Yes, I thought, one would probably never need glasses without the television and the cinema and smog – if one didn't die of pneumonia through the elements.

She commented on my wet hair: 'You must not be catching the cold now,' and indicated the chair opposite where I sat carefully concealing my knees. I told her about the lamb and the punctured tyre, but carefully omitted my skirmishes with the MacMhor factor. I was getting rather sensitive to ridicule and had a feeling she might rather sternly and readily take his side, especially when the girl at the barred window had also warned me off. However, I was dying to know about the strange woman who had sheltered me.

'Ach, that would be Tanoth MacMhor.'

'Tanoth. What a lovely name. Is it Gaelic?'

Gran shook her head and looked uneasily at the Bible in her hands. 'No, it is not. It is the name in the Old Religion for the Moon Goddess. She was found as a wee bairn, thirty years ago, floating on the waters in an empty boat near Eilean na Gealach and none claimed her, or knew how she got there.' She closed her mouth firmly and seemed about to change the subject, but I wanted to know more.

'Eilean na Gealach,' I said carefully. 'Aren't those the strange rocks I saw sticking out of the sea from the ferry?'

'They are. In the English it is the Isle of

51

the Moon, so that is why folk here called the babe Tanoth. She is a strange fey creature, right enough, simple some say, too, but kindly. She foresaw the death of the MacMhor's betrothed and warned him, but he took no heed. Ach, it was to be expected,' she added in a matter-of-fact way of one who has learned to accept the inevitable. 'It was ordained, for haven't the last three generations all lost their loved ones? The MacMhor's grandmother and his mother both died soon after their marriages. Of natural causes some say. Ach, to be sure, but they're an unlucky family, the MacMhors, and the luck gets worse. It is no doubt themselves to blame. In the past they were a godless, wild lot, lairds or no, womanising and such matters. Then there was that long-ago chief of the MacMhors who fell foul of a witch-woman called Rowan, and then when he wanted to marry a rich mainland woman with money, starved her to death in Castle Clodha.'

She paused and gave me a hard look. 'No doubt, of course, your father would be telling you all about the old story.'

'When I was small,' I lied in his defence,

'I seem to remember something . . .'

'Ach yes. You'll mind then how Rowan died cursing the whole family. It was a very strange thing that according to the legend she too had been rescued from the sea off Eilean na Gealach. Remembering the catastrophies she brought to the island, many would like to have seen the bairn Tanoth put back to the sea to drown, but the MacMhor said no, perhaps the wheel had turned full circle and this one would bring them luck.' She sighed. 'There has been no evidence of luck coming back to Clodha, but there were those that thought the MacMhor's heart was set on one of his sons wedding Tanoth and setting the evil right.

'But the poor lass, marriage was not for her, nor any of the normal things in life. She grew to be a woman in body but stayed a little child in her mind. Aye, many wish her ill and fear her. In the old days she would have been put back in the sea or burnt as a witch, but those who believe in the Old Religion seek her help with love potions, and spells − and many a less innocent thing, I'll be sure.'

She looked at me and something clicked

into place. The 'Old Religion' – I had been thinking she was referring to the pre-Reformation Scotland, but now I realised she was referring to the pre-Christian world, to witches and demons, and I wondered in amazement if witchcraft was also practised on Clodha. I could well believe it to be so, for the whole place gave me a feeling that it was older than time, or that time had raced ahead and left this island stranded on a silver sea.

'There's no call for you to be scared of her, a harmless creature not much older than yourself.'

'I don't think she liked me.'

'And why should you be thinking that?'

'She said something – in Gaelic.' I had discovered too late to do anything about it that I had a natural ear for languages and for all musical sounds. My written French at school was atrocious but I could hear it once and repeat it perfectly. Now as best I could I haltingly repeated the words Tanoth had spoken. As I did so I could have sworn that Gran turned pale and clutched at the blankets.

She stared at me and it was obviously a conscious effort for her to reply: 'I don't know what she meant, child,' she said hurriedly. 'You must have got the words wrong. They do not make any sense at all. Ach, listen,' she said with evident relief, 'isn't that Katrine I'm hearing downstairs? Go you and see who she has with her.'

As I went downstairs I felt cheated, knowing full well that whatever Tanoth had said certainly *did* make sense to her.

In the kitchen was Katrine's visitor, a well-groomed elegantly kilted version of the man who had let his dog terrify me and later offered me a lift in the rain. Above the savage plane of cheekbones, amber eyes gleamed gold, amiable and smilingly at home he warmed his hands at the peat fire.

'Miss May Lachlan, welcome to Clodha,' he said, bowing over my hand.

'This is Rory – er, Roderick Malcolm MacMhor, chief of the MacMhors,' said Katrine fondly, and I felt the blush of shame starting at the soles of my feet and slowly enveloping me.

Chapter Four

IF the transformation of factor into clan chieftain, charming, elegant, and bowing. over my hand, had shocked all sensible conversation out of me, I could not help noticing also the change in Katrine. Her expression indicated that this was a welcome and frequent visitor, her deliberate casualness hinting at some subtle possession and intimacy. Here then was the answer to one riddle.

Her rejection of Colin MacMhor. Poor Katrine, I thought, a woman in love, perhaps even hopelessly, and unable to hide it either, with a man already married, as I remembered the girl at the castle window.

'Rory,' she said, 'you must show May round Castle Clodha, and the home farm. She'll love the baby animals.' She took his arm, eyes glowing with pride in him.

'So you love animals, Miss Lachlan,' he said softly. 'I have a dog in the car outside, Shep's his name. Maybe you'd like to meet him.' Under the raised black wings of brows his eyes were bright, a devil in them enjoying and prolonging every moment of my embarrassment.

Furiously I stared at him, biting my lip, longing to do something violent. Then quite suddenly the feeling vanished, to be replaced by weariness utter and complete. I thought I had never been so tired in my life before. What a mistake to come to Clodha at all. I longed from the empty depths of my soul for the long impersonal street that had been home. I was bitterly homesick, swamped by a longing for the father I would never see again.

I excused myself and went to bed, where despite exhaustion — and tears — I lay awake, wondering why I had left so much that was dear — the boutique and Sarah and acquaintances made enchanting by the distance that separated us, for a grandmother who neither wanted me nor made any secret of her disapproval, for a holiday that had proved in its first day nothing more than a series of terrors, disasters and embarrassments. As I remembered especially the embarrassments in acute detail, I buried my head in the pillow and between me and sleep came the mocking provocative face of Rory MacMhor.

At last in a series of fitful dreams my first day on Clodha ended and I opened my eyes on sunlight and Grandmother's chickens in full voice below the window. A cow somewhere near urgently and mournfully pleaded to be milked and the seagulls' cries echoed like ghostly mocking laughter across an azure sky. I turned over, and Castle Clodha, Rory MacMhor's grim and ancient stronghold, stared down at me.

I sprang out of bed and the whole of last night's pageant of misfortunes seemed absurd. As I threw open the window and breathed in the wine-clear air I thought of London sounds. The milkman whistling, bottle-banging his way from door to door. The early-morning bus tearing along the street. Gates banging, feet running, children shouting, a jet screaming overhead. Hustle, bustle, smells of diesel oil . . .

I sniffed the air again. Oh, what heaven to look out on the blue of heather, the yellow gorse, the bright green of pasture land after rain, with here and there the quilted look of fields under crops. All of Clodha seemed to rest in a silver setting and far to the horizons stretched the deep sapphire sea.

At breakfast Katrine said we would walk down to the village where she would show me round without the disasters of a punctured bicycle.

'That would be lovely, but I don't want to keep you from your work.'

She smiled, hands on hips. 'What work? My dear girl, my work for the day is almost over. I've been up and about since six, although Rory and I didn't get home until midnight.'

I wondered what they found to do until midnight on Clodha, but was too polite to enquire. The statement seemed rather brash, I thought, if Rory was married. Perhaps the girl I had seen was sister or servant?

'And what do you think of him?' asked Katrine softly.

'I've been wondering how on earth I'd ever face him again after dismissing him as one of the castle servants.'

Katrine laughed. 'Yes, he told me. He thought it was a huge joke. After all, you must try and see it from his angle. You were a stranger to him and you do sound so very English – and believe me they're not a race he has much time for. So how could he be anything but suspicious when he found you in such compromising circumstances?' She paused. 'You haven't answered my question. Do you like him?' she insisted.

'He seemed very nice,' I said generously, and Katrine nodded approvingly.

We walked down the hill silently for a moment or two then she asked: 'Have you ever been in love, May? I don't mean to pry but I thought perhaps you had a boy back home.'

I thought of the 'gang'. Sarah's arty friends, the parties, the dates, the discos. The importance of being someone's 'steady', the small intrigues and jealousies. The Pop world of trendy fashions, permissive sex, where the unforgivable was to be square.

'No, there isn't anyone special just now.' And Rory MacMhor's mocking face drifted before me. Rory who was probably married and at thirty would surely be The Squarest in the eyes of absent friends and acquaintances.

'Really?' said Katrine with a smile. 'I

thought everyone in London belonged to a swinging set.'

'Maybe I'm getting too old for the swinging set and in fact I've had very little time to spare since Dad was ill.'

I told her about my father and she nodded sympathetically. 'You look very young, May. How old are you – may I ask?' When I told her twenty-three, she shrugged and said: 'Oh, you've plenty of time yet to fall in love.'

Plenty of time. Still it sometimes scared me as I watched other girls and boys in the 'gang' pair off, get married and I began to feel like an old-timer when the first babies came along. Why did my own heart never awaken or know more than fleeting desire?

Katrine's words frightened me. Was I going to be one of those despairing frigid women who write to the agony columns of magazines, pretending at love and inheriting disaster by marrying without it? The countless thousands who never know the ecstasies and joys of real love or real surrender.

'What about yourself?' I asked. Katrine looked dazzling this morning, with her long black hair blowing in the breeze, her

61

striking good looks, radiant in the morning sun.

'Och well, it is as I told you yesterday. I cannot really make up my mind.' She frowned. 'You see there is Colin and there is Rory, and I don't know who to choose.'

'Rory isn't married then?'

She laughed. 'Of course not. Whatever made you think that?'

Well, if she didn't know about the girl in Castle Clodha, I wasn't going to be the one to tell her, and leaving my heart to sort out the dark flood of delight at the news that Rory MacMhor was unattached, I said: 'Oh, a castle seems rather large to live in alone.' I expected to be told he had relatives, sisters, servants.

Katrine shook her head. 'He manages somehow. I look in a couple of times a week and keep an eye on things.'

Not very effectively, I thought, deciding that Rory played a very crafty game as I wondered how he kept Miss Red-Gold Hair out of Miss Jealous Katrine Lachlan's way.

Outside Colin MacMhor's garage, a tall slim man with black straight hair blowing into his eyes was throwing a suitcase into the back seat of a handsome red sports car. My heart raced. There was something familiar . . .

He turned round and smiled. It was Colin not Rory, after all.

Katrine waved. 'Hello, Colin. And where are you off to?' she demanded coyly.

'Glasgow,' he replied, looking anxiously to where the ferry waited. 'Got to see a man about an engine.'

'Oh, is that all?'

'Well, it's all I'm telling you,' said Colin with a grin.

Katrine laughed. 'Colin's building a new speedboat down there in the harbour. Having trouble?'

'Plenty of that, aye. Seeing as she's your namesake, Katrine Lachlan, it is all I can expect from her.'

'What cheek,' said Katrine, looking pleased.

A warning toot from the ferry's horn and he sprang into the car. 'Cheerio and be good.' He gave me a large wink as he drove past. 'Don't do anything I wouldn't do, girls.'

'He's a great character,' said Katrine.

'I'm really very fond of him. It's so difficult. You see, there's Rory too. And to make matters worse they absolutely loathe one another. It's a matter of inheritance – believe you me, all troubles on this island always stem from money or property. Anyway, Rory is hereditary chief of the MacMhors and, of course, Colin believes he should be . . .'

Unfortunately this interesting conversation was interrupted by an arm waving out of a car to Katrine who rushed over. A large red-faced woman had an animated conversation with her, meanwhile eyeing me curiously over Katrine's shoulder.

'That was Meg MacMhor, the district nurse, wanting her eggs – and a good look at you,' Katrine chuckled. 'If you hadn't walked on, you would have been introduced and there we would have been stuck for the next two hours while she delved deep into all your family history.'

'Another MacMhor, and what relation is she to Colin and – his cousin?'

'Cousin remote,' said Katrine. 'Look at the names above the shops here. You see, they're nearly all MacMhors or Lachlans, or folk related to us by marriage. The Lachlans were always privileged. In the old clan-raising days Lachlan was the hereditary piper of the MacMhor and preceded him into battle. There isn't really very much here to draw newcomers. It's the same sad story on the mainland too, but here the Lachlans and MacMhors feel a real sense of betrayal when their young men depart for other places, almost as if they abandoned the clan mid-battle.'

And that, I thought, explained my grandmother's withdrawn attitude to her son going to London and her treatment of her grand-daughter as a stranger and foreigner. I was learning a lot this morning. I also had the answer to why an attractive girl like Katrine Lachlan could bear to waste her life on a chicken farm, all for a slender hope that some day she might marry Rory and be wife to the chief.

I wondered aloud was there enough to support the young people who stayed and Katrine said: 'Fishing, sheep and cattle-farming – a few crops and not much else. Colin has some grand ideas of turning the island into a holiday camp and making hay while summer and the tourists come, but not many agree with him. They want to keep it unspoilt, besides Clodha throws out a strange' – the word came reluctantly I thought – 'magic and Lachlans and MacMhors rarely settle happily away from their own land.' For a moment I thought her face darkened. 'There are, of course, some MacMhors in Perthshire.'

Below us on the quayside several fishing boats, big, well painted and prosperous-looking, were unloading their catch to a screaming chorus of gulls who pursued with angry cries the crane busily transferring the baskets of fish to the Oban ferry.

Katrine looked at her watch. 'The ferry's late leaving this morning. It had to wait for the boats arriving. They almost didn't make it at all after last night's storm. They had to wait until the seas around Eilean na Gealach died down.' And when I remarked on the size of the catch she said: 'It's not all for eating now, most goes for curing and fishmeal on the mainland.'

The fishing boats all had MacMhor in their names. 'They're all Colin's, named for his family. In fact, I was very honoured to have the speedboat named for me.'

66

'He must be very fond of you.'

'Oh, he is,' she said with a rather indifferent shrug, as I followed her into Lachlan's General Store and stood waiting while she made her purchases, chatting in Gaelic to another Mrs Lachlan behind the counter, who shook my hand with a greeting in careful English.

Katrine departed for a few moments to deliver some eggs to a bedridden friend of Grandmother's and I stood idly contemplating the shop windows. I had never realised that Clodha would enjoy the benefits of television commercials and had some idea they would still be making their own soap. But there before me was the guarantee of a whiter wash next Monday.

Aware of someone close by, I turned, and there was Tanoth MacMhor. Her greeting in Gaelic was gentle enough and so was her smile. With the sunshine glittering on the sea and the busy scene at the quay, I wondered why I had ever thought of her as sinister. Long pale hair blowing, her face was that of a guileless lovely child, nearer ten years old than thirty. I wondered sadly what tragedy somewhere, somehow before she was born, had sealed her into eternal childhood. What parent could have so cruelly put out a baby to drown in an empty boat near the terrible rocks at Eilean na Gealach?

She spoke again and from behind her back proudly produced a tiny bunch of flowers. Pink, yellow, blue, far removed from the buttercups and daisies which were the limits of my town-dweller's knowledge of wild flowers. When I thanked her and said: 'How kind of you,' her trilling laugh of pleasure was a small girl's. Remembering the woman in the cottage in the rain, pointing at me and murmuring words which had certainly frightened Gran, remembering those eerie pale faces watching from the tapestry with the woman with red-gold hair from Castle Clodha in their midst, it was impossible to imagine this pretty innocent-seeming girl connected with possible witchcraft and other stranger affairs. . . .

I was having doubts about Tanoth's 'powers' when Katrine appeared round the corner. To say that Tanoth practically leaped into the air would not be the slightest exaggeration. Her eyes were wide with horror and she seemed to back away from Katrine in terror and revulsion.

Katrine too looked shaken by this encounter. There was an odd expression quite unfathomable in her eyes as she looked from Tanoth to me and back again. It wasn't until much later I realised what that expression meant. She was afraid of Tanoth.

But Tanoth was away, disappearing down the little street, hurrying through a gate leading towards the hill, like a child caught robbing an orchard.

Katrine turned, her smile rather uneven. 'And what on earth did that daft creature want with you?'

I held out the flowers and she turned rather pale. 'Good heavens, May,' she said, struggling to keep her voice normal, 'you must be popular. Those flowers only grow away down the cliff-face, over there.' I looked where she pointed, a sheer drop from the castle to the jagged black rocks in the sea.

I sniffed the flowers. 'Smell them, Katrine. They've a lovely perfume.'

But Katrine shied away from them as if there might be dynamite inside. 'I wouldn't keep them. Throw them away, May. Throw them away.' There was a note of rising hysteria in her voice now. 'Nothing Tanoth MacMhor gives you will ever bring luck.'

I had no intention of throwing away the pretty posy, so neatly arranged, just to please Katrine. The episode with Tanoth had certainly frightened her. I tried to understand why and said: 'Aren't you being a little hard on her?'

'Hard. I suppose you think she's kind and harmless, the way Gran does. Oh, if you only knew ... She's horrible, wicked and utterly evil. People — people like her ought to be put down painlessly.' Her eyes gleamed. 'In the old days she would have been burnt as a witch.'

I laughed. 'Katrine — for goodness' sake. This is the twentieth century. Surely you don't believe in all that nonsense.'

Katrine pulled the cellophane off a cigarette packet and threw it away in an angry gesture. 'I just wish I never had to set eyes on her again, that's all. Anyway,' she added sharply, 'I don't know why you're taking her side. I gather from Gran she frightened you when you took shelter in the rain.'

'Did Gran tell you what she said to me?'

'No, she didn't, except that it was in Gaelic, something you didn't understand.'

'I can remember the words clearly, Katrine. Gran said she didn't know what they meant, but perhaps you do.' Some of the words had faded from my memory, but I repeated what I could remember.

Katrine stopped. 'Are you sure that's what she said?' she asked, her voice hushed, afraid.

'Most of it. What does it mean?'

'Oh, nothing – just a warning, that's all.' Katrine avoided my eyes and began walking briskly back towards the cottage.

I seized her arm. 'Tell me, Katrine. I'm not worried. I'm not superstitious, I don't believe in fortune-telling, curses or bad luck. We generally bring about our own misfortunes, without any help from the stars.'

'Are you sure you want to know?'

'Yes.'

'Very well then. She said something like: "Evil comes – danger – death – you will die on Clodha".' I must have turned pale, for she grasped my arm. 'You insisted on knowing, I'm sorry. Cheer up, May, you must have got it wrong. I'm sure she couldn't know – I mean, wouldn't say – that. Actually, the Gaelic is so easy to misunderstand . . .'

I followed her slowly up the hill. Gaelic might be easy to misunderstand but the impact of Tanoth's fateful words were unmistakable. And as for the premonition of danger, I realised I hadn't needed her prophecy. I had known all along, waiting in an empty house in a London suburb two days ago. It had begun there. Before I set foot on Clodha.

Before my destiny led me to Rory MacMhor.

Chapter Five

AFTER Katrine's interpretation of Tanoth's strange words was it only fancy that she was rather insistent on not letting me out of her sight? When we reached home she had a long consultation – in Gaelic – with Gran upstairs and when we had lunch did I only imagine they had both taken refuge in a determined-to-be-kind, hearty manner, as if they had learned I had something incurable and wanted at all costs to keep the truth from me?

As we washed the dishes, Katrine announced: 'How about coming to Castle Clodha with me? You can have a look around while I tidy up – it's my day for looking in on Rory. If you're too tired to walk, we'll take the car,' she added with anxious consideration.

My reluctance came from the prospect of meeting Rory. However, it seemed likely we'd be encountering each other with fair constancy during my stay, so I had better get used to it. The first time would be worst.

'I'd enjoy the walk,' I said, remembering Katrine's erratic and impulsive driving from the harbour and with little desire to see it in action on that steep and murderous cliff road where a bicycle was hard enough to steer.

As we left, Gran followed us to the door and said to Katrine in English: 'Now you be staying with her, do you hear?' And to me with a rather wan smile: 'She will take

73

good care of you, May. You will be safe with Katrine.'

'I'm sure I will.' And determined to show how little worried I was by Tanoth MacMhor and her dire prophecy, I began a spirited talk about Sarah's boutique and what was in fashion with my London friends.

Katrine listened with great enthusiasm. 'You do have lovely hair,' said Katrine. 'I suppose it's naturally red?' She sighed. 'You're lucky not to have inherited the Clodha brand of Indian straight black hair.'

'But I think your hair is gorgeous, Katrine. I love black hair.'

'We never do get the looks we want, do we?' said Katrine and we both laughed, a new bond growing between us. 'It must be heaven living in London – all the shops, the theatres ...'

'Once I've found a place to live of my own, perhaps you'll come for a visit some summer.'

'I'd love that, I could always get someone to look after Gran for a week. I'd maybe find all sorts of things to improve my looks in London.'

'You don't need them, Katrine. No, I'm not flattering you, honestly. Your eyes, complexion, hair – and your figure. Did you never fancy modelling? After all, Glasgow isn't all that far away.'

'I did go away once, I suppose with some idea like that in mind. I was sick fed up of Clodha and everyone on it. A couple of years ago, I went to Glasgow. Perhaps I even had some hopes of finding a husband and settling down away from the island. Well, men I found in plenty, willing to employ me in shops or as a waitress, but they all suffered from roving hands and one day I decided there wasn't any glamour in the big city at close quarters. Once you're an islander, it's too hard trying to live – to adjust to the city. Everything and everybody moves too fast.'

I remembered Dad, how he had hated London, enduring a hard wearying job and life in a suburban street, just to make life pleasanter for Mother and me.

'Then I met a fellow who worked in insurance,' Katrine continued. 'He had a good job, his family were what we on the island would call very comfortably off. He asked me to marry him. I said yes and the very next day I lost my nerve and came back here to Clodha. Suddenly I saw it all very clearly. The island – and the people. Everything I really loved and wanted was right here and I couldn't bear the thought of spending the rest of my life in some alien place.'

Far below us now a pretty harbour with a few shops and houses, a garage, school, church. All very attractive in a modest way, enough to remember nostalgically from a summer holiday, but only an excellent and pressing reason would make any girl want to devote her life to it. Especially a girl with Katrine's looks. Anyone could have looked after Gran in this closely knit society – and run the chicken farm.

And although I had never been in love myself, still I believed romantically that nothing – no place on earth – could compete with a man's love. Had Katrine loved the man in Glasgow she would have gone with him without a qualm or a backward glance to the other end of the world.

No, the answer wasn't Clodha or Colin's fine garage and fishing boats. I looked up at the grim outline of Castle Clodha growing nearer, with its turrets peeping through the spinney. Rory MacMhor. The answer was there. He was the magnet that had drawn Katrine back . . .

And there was Katrine explaining it all, the obvious reason for her departure. 'Rory had returned from the funeral of a MacMhor who lived in a castle in Perthshire. Not a castle like this, but elegant and still going strong. There was money and an only daughter Isobel and he brought her back for a holiday. The next thing we knew he was engaged. There was nowhere grand enough for her to stay in the village, so she took her servants and moved into the Castle. All the plans for the wedding were made. She asked me to be bridesmaid and a week after I returned from Glasgow she was dead. Perhaps if I had gone to stay in the Castle, as she asked me to – we were friends – it might never have happened. I could have warned her. Apparently nobody else did, not even Rory.'

'What happened?'

Katrine looked at me and said slowly:

'You wondered why I wanted you to throw those flowers away this morning, the ones Tanoth gave you? Well, Isobel loved wild flowers, she had studied botany.' And smiling as if she saw her quite clearly, she continued: 'For all her university degree, she was not the kind of wife you'd imagine for a man as handsome as Rory. Quiet and frail-looking. Clever, but so useless at housework she had to bring her retinue of servants to Clodha. She had never done anything for herself. Anyway, one day she was gathering flowers on the cliffside, she missed her footing — and that was that.'

I shuddered. It was a long way down to hurtle to rocks that looked black, sharp and evil. Nobody could possibly survive such a fall.

'We thought Rory would go mad with remorse. People, of course, started remembering the MacMhor curse coming home to roost and reminding themselves that hadn't Rory's grandmother and mother both died soon after marriage, although childbirth and drowning would appear to be natural causes. There were those who thought Tanoth's presence brought about this new disaster, but Rory

78

laughed and said such talk belonged to the dark ages, that the deaths in his family were pure coincidence. When Isobel died, the Perthshire MacMhor money came to him, although their castle and the title went to a closer cousin in the south of Scotland.

'The money at least was a godsend, for Rory was facing disaster and it looked as if he would have to sell out to this holiday camp as Colin wanted, if he was not to face bankruptcy.'

'What was Isobel like – to look at?'

'Little, bird-like, plain.'

'Did she have red hair?'

'Heavens no, nothing so striking.' Katrine gave me a puzzled look. 'She had brown hair and was very short-sighted, wore glasses all the time. A lovely voice, but nobody looking at her would have thought she was heiress to a title or to money, believe me. Now what made you imagine she had red hair?'

'I don't know, just an idea. What about the MacMhor curse – do you think it's a lot of nonsense?'

Katrine shrugged. 'Many strange things have happened – and do happen – on Clodha, which can't be explained away by natural causes. When you live as close to the elements as we do here you come to rely on sympathetic magic — what used to be called "placating the gods", if you like. In towns it would be dismissed as superstition, but here we just walk carefully — when the sea can spring up and take a man or a woman's life, when a storm can destroy his sheep or ruin his crops. I've learned that it is never a good thing to scoff at magic, or to tempt fate unnecessarily. We go this way ...'

Following her across the stile, I discovered we were back on the road by the spinney, the scene of my first encounter with Rory MacMhor. Even the farm looked prosperous and busy this afternoon. Yesterday's derelict abandoned appearance might have belonged to a strange nightmare.

We took a path to the right, through a small belt of firs and emerged at the front of Castle Clodha where, far above our heads, the St. Andrew's flag, streaming forth into the wind, announced that the chief of MacMhors was in residence. Despite smooth lawns around us, which reached up to the castle walls, it was a grim dour-looking building, most of the windows narrow, built more with an eye to defence than to comfort. But judging by size alone, the MacMhors had once been a large and powerful family. As we walked to the ancient oak door, mounds of stone covered by grass indicated the presence of earlier buildings which had perished through time's passing.

'This is the only wing in use now,' said Katrine, thrusting open the seven-foot-high door, surmounted by the crumbling stone relic of a coat of arms. 'The castle's falling into disuse, despite all Rory does.'

A whitewashed passage disappeared into a flagged kitchen and I followed her up a narrow spiral staircase, emerging into an enormous gallery where a large stone fireplace yawned. Antique furniture lined the walls and portraits stared down on us. At one end a large arched window gazed down across the sea towards Eilean na Gealach. 'This window was the door in the original castle, twelve feet above the ground, so that they could quell invaders. The lower floor at that time was used to keep in cattle and other animals in times of invasion. When the warning bell sounded, or the horn, the women and children were given shelter in Castle Clodha, until danger was over.

I looked around the great hall. 'How lovely it is.' I sniffed the air appreciatively. There was the mysterious fragrance of bygone ages, the very substance of time itself one met with in ancient churches. Whatever strife they had once witnessed – a witch's curse and battles long ago – the atmosphere of these stone walls was strangely at peace.

Across the gallery and through an arched recess in the stone was another door. Katrine tapped on it. 'Rory – are you there?'

There was no reply and she opened the door. 'This is the Laird's study,' she said, as I followed her into a small panelled room where under a mantelpiece adorned by Scottish flags and heraldic bearings a peat fire smouldered, bright and fragrant. Opposite the door, one tall window looked down on Clodha village.

'Isn't that the side of Gran's house we're seeing?'

'Yes. That's our bedroom.' Katrine

went back into the gallery, her voice echoing as she called: 'Ro—ry, Ro—ry.'

This was a man's room, I decided, vaguely untidy with bookshelves everywhere. Books lined the walls, sprouted on sill and tables. In one corner an old-fashioned roll-top writing desk was covered with framed photos. This study was a room meant to be lived in, faded, shabby but still elegant. A leather armchair, large and comfortable-looking, showed where the Laird's head had rested, beside it on a small table a discarded pipe and a book on Scottish history. The scene could have fitted anywhere within the last two centuries but for the telephone on the table. And, as a concession to gracious living, a silver tray and Georgian silver coffee pot, plus the masculine touch of an earthenware mug. My fingers brushed lightly against the silver pot. It was cold.

'Where is the man?' demanded Katrine indignantly, and vanished through a panelled door quite invisible at first sight. It fitted neatly into the wall and opened on to another spiral stair faintly lit by an upper window.

'Ro—ry.' There was no answer. 'The bedrooms and the rest of the livable part of the castle are up there.' She turned to me, closing the door. 'I can't imagine what has happened to him. Wait here and I'll just run down to the farm. Make yourself at home.'

She hurried out and I wondered why she didn't use the telephone to track him down until I realised she was obviously keen to find him on her own.

Alone in this warm welcoming room, I inspected the bookshelves. Historical novels, Scottish history and biography, archaeology, such was Rory MacMhor's taste in literature. One section of the wall was devoted to ancient leather-backed volumes, with Latin titles and pages yellowed with age.

The photographs on the desk were mostly family groups, here and there distinguished by a royal signed portrait, visitors to Castle Clodha in its more prosperous days earlier in the century.

I picked up a miniature in a gold frame, of a girl with red-gold hair, whose face I recognised from the window in the turret. Again I wondered at Katrine's remarkable restraint and at Rory's skill in keeping the rivals apart. Or were both women cleverer than he, each able to maintain her position in Rory's life by an elaborate pretence that the other did not exist.

Suddenly the warmth of the room made me drowsy. I was glad to sit down in the huge leather armchair, thankful to be alone in this quiet peaceful place. If these stone walls could talk, what stories, what ancient MacMhor voices would I hear, raised in anger, laughter, or soft in passion? The glowing fire and I were the only living things in the world. I was dreaming dreaming . . .

The panelled door in the wall opposite opened and a girl with red-gold hair looked in at me and smiled:

'So May has come at last? We have been waiting for you. Why did you take so long? So long . . .?'

My head jerked upwards. I was fully awake.

'Sorry – am I disturbing you?'

The girl had gone and where she had been Rory stood smiling. I sprang to my feet in embarrassment.

'No, please, do sit down. You look so at home. Yes, Miss May Lachlan,' he said, his head bent towards me, 'I had the strange feeling that the girl who looked so at home in the spinney yesterday, with one of my lambs in her arms, might also look at home sitting by my hearth.'

'I'm – sorry,' I said, my face scarlet, unsure whether he was teasing or no. 'Katrine is looking for you.'

He raised a dark eyebrow towards the gallery. 'I am well aware of that. I saw her from my bedroom window upstairs, going across to the farm. Never trouble about Katrine, she likes to pretend I need looking after, so I humour her a little. We both know, I think' – again there was that gentle mocking smile – 'that it is just a game. I'm well able to look after myself.'

There was a scratching at the door behind him. 'That'll be Shep.' As he opened the door, I sprang to my feet and Rory laughed as the dog bounded over, tail swinging. 'Don't be scared, he's really as gentle as that lamb you rescued. Paw for Miss May, Shep. Paw, boy.' A paw was duly extended and accepted. 'Now die for the lady, Shep.' He rolled over on his back and when I had scratched his chest he sprang up and very politely retreated back to Rory's feet. 'Come and see the rest of the house,' said Rory. 'Watch the stairs, they're rather worn.'

I took the hand he extended and answered his smile. With a joyous dog bounding ahead we were friends. Suddenly he stopped, and still holding my hand looked down into my eyes.

'You should smile more often, May Lachlan. Laughter becomes you,' he said softly, opening the door in front of us. 'This is the Laird's bedroom.' A panelled room, like the study directly below it, but very much larger, with a fine carved ceiling and on a raised dais a four-poster bed.

Rory leaned forward through the bed hangings and struck a match. On the elaborately carved oak headboard, above the MacMhor coat of arms, was the date:

'Fifteen-forty-three,' he read. 'Our beautiful unfortunate Mary, Queen of

Scots, was a baby still, running laughing perhaps through the corridors of Linlithgow Palace when this bed was made.' For a moment he was silent and in the small flickering light his profile belonged to a medieval painting – or was it a tapestry? Imagination painted a white ruff at his neck . . .

'Most of my family were born in that bed.'

I followed him along the corridor and he opened the door into other bedrooms, situated directly above the gallery. They were comfortable though ancient, beautifully furnished in the style of two centuries ago, but none so grand as the Laird's bedroom.

At the end of the corridor he indicated another spiral staircase and once more taking my hand led the way to where an oak door creakily opened into a small dark room.

'The turret room.'

It was empty but for a spinning wheel, a broken-down old chair covered in tapestry, a footstool. . . . But this room had a completely different atmosphere to the other rooms we had visited. Hard to explain, except that it wasn't *friendly*.

I was aware of Rory's eyes watching me intently. 'You don't like it either, do you? Strange, but nobody does. This was the room where an ancestor of mine kept a lady captive. He starved her to death, because she was having his child and he didn't want to marry her, his eyes on a richer mainland bride. This room was never used, it was always supposed to be haunted. Then in Victorian days a larger family made extra space necessary.' He touched the wooden mantelpiece. 'This monstrosity was a concession to the poor timorous maids who had to sleep here — to cover the original fireplace where Rowan left scratched in the stone her curse on the MacMhors.

> 'MacMhor betrayed and murdered me
> Accursed from now MacMhor shall
> be . . .'

He turned smiling: 'Do we seem a very odd lot after your swinging London friends?'

I laughed. 'In a very nice way you do.' I looked at him resting an arm along the mantelshelf. 'Tell me, did Rowan have red-gold hair?'

'She had.'

I walked over to the window and looked down through its bars into the spinney where I had wrestled with my lamb while she had watched me from this room . . .

'You've met her already.' I turned and Rory was beside me, my hair touching his shoulder. 'So you have the Sight, May Lachlan.' I didn't answer. 'Come on, admit it. You nearly scared the wits out of me yesterday with all that talk about my mistress seeing you rescue the lamb – until I realised it must be Rowan you were seeing. Was I right?'

'Yes. And I saw her again – or dreamed it, I'm not quite sure, just before you came into the study.'

'You saw her all right. It was no dream. The stairs were unnaturally cold. They're always like that when she's around.'

'I don't know. I *thought* I was dreaming.'

'You're like all those with the Sight, aren't you? Afraid of it, ashamed to admit that there are more things in heaven and earth than can be proved by science?'

'It's something I would rather *not* have.'

He gave me a strange look. 'Some day you may be very glad.'

'Have you ever seen her?'

He hesitated. 'Yes, once. She is not a welcome sight to the MacMhor, she brings death or disaster.' His eyes had taken on a brooding, far-away expression. His face was tight-lipped, shut in, as silently he closed the door and led the way downstairs, I felt the coldness too, as if between us, all the warmth, the friendliness had faded.

Chapter Six

THE Laird's study waited, glowing and inviting. It was like stepping into another world. Rory took the miniature off the writing desk and held it out.

'Was this the girl you saw?' When I

nodded, he said: 'That was Rowan,' and replacing it carefully on the desk: 'It's believed to be a good likeness.'

Turning, he held out his hands. 'You look cold, May Lachlan, you must not let Castle Clodha's ghosts make you uneasy. Come then to the fire.' Smiling, he added: 'I am not a very good host, taking you on a chilly – and chilling tour ...'

'Don't apologise, I'm glad you did. Castle Clodha – it's enchanting. Imagine living in such a place, so old, so much history. Do you know the house I lived in all my life until last week was built in 1930 and the people talked rather proudly of it as being "pre-war" – *that* was beginning to sound like history.'

'Tell me about it.'

'There's precious little to tell. One enormously long street. We were number 256, right next to the bus-stop. Half an hour's ride from the heart of London.'

'Well, I expect for the English, London has its romance,' said Rory with a frown, as if he doubted it. 'Edinburgh affects me the same way,' he added kindly. 'When I was a student there years ago I lodged in a terrace house built in 1886. That seemed very dashing and modern after the castle, I might tell you.' He looked at me thoughtfully, eyes that could smoulder darkly, now golden and kind. 'I hope you won't be disappointed in Clodha. There is little to do for a girl alone on a summer holiday.'

'But I love it. The sea, the air – oh, everything.' His look was so intent, I felt suddenly shy. 'I expect it's very lonely in winter.'

'My dear girl, I grew up to loneliness, as you call it. I became Chieftain after Grandfather died when I was eighteen. He brought me up to inherit, to recognise responsibility. My father and uncle were both killed in action during the war and Mother had died in a sailing accident off Eilean na Gealach before I could clearly remember her. There are things harder to bear than loneliness, and being alone is not quite the same as being lonely. Aloneness is often from choice.' He smiled. 'After all, I am very fortunate, I have my island, the home farm to keep me occupied, and I dabble in politics too. After all that, if I find time hangs heavy there are my books and Shep here. And of course,' he added gravely, 'my friend Katrine who likes to think she takes care of me.'

He stood up. 'Ah, talking of Katrine, at this very moment she is probably searching for the coffee pot here and worrying about having deserted you . . .'

At that the door opened and Katrine entered. 'And where have you been, Rory MacMhor, playing hide-and-seek? There am I, slaving away in your kitchen after searching outside for you, and you sneak past and never say a word . . .' She went on, pretending to be angry, making him laugh and protest. But occasionally she darted a curious glance in my direction and I felt uncomfortably aware that Katrine was not at all pleased by the turn of events. Poor Katrine, she would have enjoyed showing me round at Rory's side, for a brief moment basking in the vicarious glory of being his devoted friend and perhaps, who knows, a whisper in her heart – of being the MacMhor's lady some day.

As we went through the gallery, downstairs to the front door, Rory took my arm gently: 'I'll just get my and May can pretend I'm a sheph the factor and rail at me too. The have had the pleasure of meeting shrews in less than twenty-four hours.'

The blush on my cheek wasn't entirely due to the warm firm hand on my arm and his teasing smile. There was a quality about Rory MacMhor I had never encountered in any other man, something strange and wonderful that stirred my blood. The power of the MacMhor, of Castle Clodha, as factor or as Laird.

As we shook hands outside the great door, he said: 'I wish you a fine holiday on Clodha, May Lachlan.' Turning to Katrine he added, 'Who knows, maybe she won't want to leave us when the magic of Clodha rubs off on her?'

Katrine said sharply: 'Stop mocking, Rory MacMhor, it's dangerous to scoff at magic.'

I looked at them. A jet plane screamed over our heads, leaving a white tracer in the cloudless blue sky. This was the twentieth century at least up there it was, but down here? I wasn't sure. The world

...ad known all my life was already retreating, perhaps for ever. The winds of Clodha brought a new dimension, a new awareness into my life. Something – or someone – with the irresistible power of a magnet.

But was it Clodha that had the magic, or the castle with its ghost of the witch a MacMhor had once betrayed? Or the strange girl, Tanoth? Or was it all easier to explain, a much more prosaic solution, that there was magic in first love, in the first stirrings of the heart for a man of flesh-and-blood and strange power – Rory MacMhor, with his brooding good looks and his eyes like a loch in sunshine after a storm?

Involved by my thoughts, I must have walked down the steep cliff road and talked to Katrine, a normal conversation about the holiday, for she said:

'Two weeks will soon pass.'

Her words brought back sane reality and panic slid through me like a cloud over a sunny sky. After all, wasn't I expecting far too much? I was only a holidaymaker, an English tourist – a foreigner in the eyes of Clodha, despite my Lachlan blood. Neither Clodha nor, to be honest, Rory MacMhor could be considered on a permanent basis.

London was my world, Sarah's boutique its orbit and a flat, shared with Sarah and her family, my ultimate foreseeable future. Whatever magic Clodha contained was a passing experience, something to be relished now and laughed about – all except the ghost of Rowan – in years to come. I thought urgently of taking photographs, some tangible record I could paste in an album and remember with nostalgia in the years ahead. By next year I would be thinking what a fool I'd been – a holiday romance was all it had meant. Romance? Common sense told me it wasn't even that. Rory was not *my* romance. Katrine clearly indicated to anyone interested that she considered him very much her property.

And at that moment Fate in the prosaic exterior of Clodha's postman, Sandy Lachlan, came toiling up the hill and handed over two letters. In Gran's cottage we opened them. Mine was from Sarah, hoping the holiday was super and enclosing a letter which she said was 'from your mysterious elderly suitor who has been calling at the boutique regularly since you went away. I didn't want to give him your address on holiday in case his intentions weren't honourable, but he says he's a friend of the family, so I hope it's all right.'

Completely mystified, I opened the letter. 'Dear May, The news of your father's death was a great shock to me I offer rather late my deepest sympathy. He was a good man and a true friend, who long ago saved me from the terrible consequences of my folly by giving me every penny he had. We were both young then but I have never forgotten. I am pleased to tell you I can now repay that debt ten-fold, for life in South America has been kind to me. Please let me know when and where I can meet you. . . .' It was signed 'Jim Scott'.

Jim Scott. The name, common as it was, stirred a vague childhood memory. My parents sitting by the fire, an urgent whispered conversation. The words 'police' and 'prison' which had frightened me. . . .

At the other side of the table Katrine flung down her letter impatiently. 'Remember I told you after my stepfather, your Uncle Donald, died, Mother, who had qualified as a nurse, returned to Glasgow and took a job with a Scots family who went to Persia. Well, they're in Britain for a holiday and Mother wants me to go to Glasgow and see her.

'Oh how lovely for you. How long is it since you saw her?'

Katrine bit her lip, ignoring the question, and from her face I realised with some surprise that she found the prospect neither lovely nor exciting. 'Oh, what a nuisance.'

Giving her the benefit of the doubt, perhaps her conscientious looking after Gran made her regard her mother's visit in the light of being a nuisance, I asked:

'Can't she come to Clodha?'

Katrine shook her head. 'No. Her name is forbidden in this house. Gran threw her out when she decided to go to Glasgow, seemed to consider Mother had no right to leave Clodha even as a widow.' She laughed bitterly. 'Gran's pretty rigid in her conventions. Once you belong to Clodha or to the Lachlans, only death can part you from them.'

Probably Gran was remembering the bitter experience of learning that young people who go — like my father — rarely ever return.

'I suppose I'll have to go. Haven't seen her for three — no, four years.'

'She'll be looking forward to meeting you after such a long time.'

Katrine shrugged indifferently. 'Perhaps. Though Mother and I never were particularly close. I expect she *feels* it's a duty to see me. She was happy enough to abandon me here with Gran at the earliest opportunity, I can tell you. They always got on each other's nerves.'

No wonder her mother was glad to escape! How appalling to be confined to a bickering existence with someone on a place the size of Clodha. How sad, too, when parents and children drift so far apart, I thought, remembering how happy and united my own family background had always been.

Katrine slammed dishes on to the table, wearing the sullen and displeased expression already familiar when things weren't going the way she wanted them to. I suspected that behind that pretty face Katrine lacked a warm heart and saved her dazzling qualities for the people she really wanted to charm, like Colin and Rory.

'Mother has all the luck,' said Katrine, 'twice my age and seeing the world. They're going to Hong Kong next — while here I am stuck on Clodha for the rest of my life. Not that I envy her nursing, that would bore me terribly. When she asks me in letters what I'm doing now I always reply: "Just the same as always." You can bet that her first question when we meet will be: "Haven't you found a husband yet, dear?" And when I tell her no, she'll sigh and say: "You're getting on, Katrine. Time you found someone. Why, I had been married twice by the time I was your age." '

How awful, I thought, picturing them together. Mother and daughter without a single bond in common, except the accident of birth.

'Oh, come now, Katrine. Won't you

enjoy seeing all the bright lights of Glasgow again? And you'll be able to tell her about Colin and Rory, and that you can't decide...'

'Oh, that. She won't be interested – it's old history. Colin's been chasing me since I was fourteen.'

'What about Rory?' My voice seemed to go noticeably small.

'It's only since Isobel's death that he's seemed interested. I expect he's just lonely.' She was silent for a moment and I couldn't think of anything to say, except to be meanly glad in my heart that he wasn't obviously in love with her and she seemed to know it.

'May, couldn't you come with me – to Glasgow?'

Quite selfishly, I hadn't the slightest intention of leaving Clodha a minute before that fatal ferry to Oban, still agreeably in the future. 'It would be fun,' I said cautiously, searching for an excuse. 'But – what about Gran? I wouldn't dare, she would be terribly offended, I'm sure.'

'Oh, I had quite forgotten Gran. Good job you reminded me. She'll need someone to look after her while I'm away.'

'I'll do that. No, honestly, it isn't any trouble at all. I'd love to stay and let you have a holiday – it's such a chance.' And all the time I felt abysmally hypocritical, because my eagerness had nothing to do with dutiful attentions to Gran.

Katrine had brightened at the prospect of Glasgow. 'And I'm sure I can get Mother to treat me to some new clothes. That'll be the second thing she'll say. "Katrine, dear, you really are looking dowdy. Why on earth don't you smarten yourself up – do something with your hair?" Useless to tell her that nobody on Clodha has ever heard of the latest fashions, what was good enough for Mother is good enough for them. That's another problem – I haven't anything to wear.'

I gave it a second's thought. 'The white coat I arrived in. You tried it on – would you like to borrow it?'

Katrine gave a delighted shriek. 'Oh, wouldn't I just? Would you really lend it to me? I'd take such good care of it.'

'You're very welcome to it.'

'Then that's settled. Do you know, I'm almost looking forward to going, although I might as well admit it,' she added with a frown, 'the role of dutiful daughter is not one I play very well.' She paused. 'I think I've shocked you just a little.'

'Not really. Parents never seem to understand when one is young and when one grows up, and is willing to try, somehow it's too late. The gap's grown too big to bridge. I was lucky, but not all my friends were.'

Katrine looked at me somehow pityingly. 'Not only you were lucky, you're still very young. You haven't yet learned that life is just a big jungle and your part in it is simply to survive. Nobody else matters, nobody else cares a damn.' Then with an abrupt change of subject: 'What was your letter about?'

'From my friend Sarah, enclosing this.'

She took the letter from Jim Scott, and read it with growing excitement. 'You are lucky, what a marvellous thing to happen. Here, he might have put you out of your agony by telling you how much.

Perhaps you're going to be an heiress.' She handed it back with: 'I'd answer that one straight away – in case he changes his mind.'

Next morning, adding natural beauty and a flair for clothes to my best coat, which had cost two weeks' salary, Katrine set out for Glasgow. As we waited for the Oban ferry to disembark, a familiar red sports car came down the ramp. Beside Colin MacMhor was a middle-aged man with a bald head and a complexion like putty, but his clothes looked elegant and his luggage expensive, covered with airline labels.

'Katrine,' said Colin, his eyes popping, 'where are you off to? – you're looking great.'

'I'm seeing my mother in Glasgow.'

Colin laughed. 'Don't look so glum. It's a great big world over there. Away from Clodha anything can happen. Go get it, girl.' To the man at his side he said: 'You've met Katrine Lachlan before, Felix – this is her cousin May from London.'

The pale eyes behind the glasses raked me over, said, 'From London, eh,' and decided that I was lacking in possibilities.

I took a rather fat clammy hand and Colin said: 'Felix Hall.'

Still holding my hand, the man said absently to Katrine: 'Nice meeting you again,' and to me, 'I'm one of your fellow-countrymen, a Sassenach in a strange land. Maybe you've heard of me: Hall Halcyon Holidays.'

Almost everyone in Britain had heard of Halcyon Holiday Camps, which operated in all the big holiday resorts. Now I knew why the man's face was vaguely familiar. I had read and seen interviews with him for the past ten years, in which he had left a trail of broken people who had the nerve or the sheer stubbornness to oppose him. A ruthless shrewd man, but one who managed, thanks to a cunning set of lawyers, to stay on the right side of the law. But only just. He had turned his attention to Katrine again.

'When are you coming south? Lovely girl like you, wasted here. I keep telling you, I'll give you a job, see you meet the right kind of people.'

Colin put an arm around her

defensively. 'And I keep telling her she's meeting the right kind of people exactly where she is.' He laughed. 'Hands off, Felix. This is my bird.'

Katrine laughed. 'Hush, Colin,' and to Felix she said sweetly: 'You never give up, do you?'

'Not when I'm on to a good thing, I don't. Felix the Foxy they call me.'

'I don't know that I would call Clodha a good thing for you, Mr. Hall.'

'Now I wonder what she can mean by that?' asked Felix in tones of mock astonishment. 'I'm here on Clodha at the personal invitation of my good friend Colin MacMhor.'

'With absolutely no thought of encountering your good enemy, Rory MacMhor, I suppose,' said Katrine gently.

The man's face went a shade paler. 'What can you be meaning? This is just a social visit, pure and simple.'

'I can't believe that you would waste your time and the furthering of Halcyon Holiday Camps on anything that was pure and simple.'

'Katrine,' said Colin heavily, 'that's

quite enough.'

Katrine turned to face him. 'Is it now? Well, you had both better keep clear of Rory MacMhor. Last time you met he practically fractured your jaw, Mr. Hall, and next time he promised he wouldn't stop at that. He told the whole island that he would kill you if you ever set foot here again. And when a MacMhor makes a public promise like that he's almost bound to keep it. So you'd better keep your guest out of his way, Colin, or there'll be murder done. Come along, May.'

'What was all that about?' I asked when we were out of earshot.

'Hall wants to buy Clodha — he's been after it for years, for a holiday camp island.' She sighed. 'And that is what has caused bad blood between Colin and Rory. You see, if Colin were chief of the MacMhor he'd sell like a shot . . .'

'Sell Clodha?'

'Yes, indeed he would. And wouldn't Colin just love all that money. Tradition means nothing to him, all he cares for are speedboats and money. Oh, I wish I wasn't going,' she said, as the warning bell sounded from the ferry. 'This could be real trouble, May, honestly, I'm not exaggerating, there will be murder if he knows Hall has come back. Hall represents everything Rory is fighting against, including Westminster and the hated Sassenach.'

And Katrine looked so worried and preoccupied it seemed inappropriate to wish her gaily: 'a good time'. As I stood on the quay waving to her, a voice asked:

'May we take you somewhere?' It was Colin.

It wasn't far to Gran's cottage, but I felt it would be churlish to refuse a lift, especially when Katrine had been rather rude and inhospitable to Felix Hall. I was sure she was letting her loyalty, her love of Rory lead her to imagine all that violence. After all, there were peaceful negotiations to settle disputes where I came from. In my innocence, as yet, I didn't dream that on an island like Clodha, men settled disputes — especially lairds who lived like feudal barons in the Middle Ages — by more violent and permanent means.

Chapter Seven

FELIX HALL made room for me beside him, but not too much room I noticed, suspecting that somehow Colin's invitation wasn't quite so innocent as it seemed. He was very interested in my London background, especially the boutique. Did I model? He had a friend who could use a good photographic model, very exclusive salary too.

I was beginning to feel rather uncomfortable, especially as Colin had taken the opposite road to Gran's cottage. Felix Hall looked and talked as if he might have the makings of a dirty old man and an ugly customer to deal with if he developed rough tactics. I felt furious with Colin for getting me into this, especially when he said:

'Once Colin shows us foreigners the layout of the island, we might be able to find the way all on our own sometime. How about it, Miss Lachlan? I'm a keen photographer too, you know,' he added with a leer that left none of his intentions to the imagination.

'I'm not a foreigner, as you call it, Mr.

Hall. My father belonged to Clodha. I'm just an exile.'

'Oh, but I have Scots blood myself. My granny came from Fife.'

I looked across at Colin. 'I'd like to go home now – please. Gran's expecting me and I have the hens to feed.'

'No tour of the island, eh.'

'Not today. I really must get back.' And I watched anxiously until he reversed the car, sitting as far away from Felix Hall as I could.

'I suppose Katrine told you Felix wants to buy Clodha,' said Colin, casually mentioning a sum double that Dad had dreamed all his life of winning in a sweepstake.

'Castle Clodha would make a perfect hotel, marvellous attraction too for American visitors. Some of the old cottages renovated, filled with antique furniture, a bit more classy than the usual holiday chalet. I might build a roadhouse and a granite house for myself ...'

'I haven't noticed many amenities on Clodha, nothing on the lines you would be accustomed to. Personally, I find it a bit primitive after London. Fine for two weeks, but to live permanently . . .'

Colin braked to a halt outside Gran's cottage and dug me in the ribs. 'Listen, child, I'm trying to sell the man Clodha and the idea that he'd like to live here. I don't need your sabotage, thanks.'

'Sell Clodha?' I said innocently. 'I'm sorry, I didn't know it was yours to sell.'

Colin gave me an angry look and an even angrier one over my shoulder in the direction of his cousin Rory's castle. 'It isn't mine — yet,' he added menacingly.

'But it soon will be,' said Felix smoothly. 'All I need to do is get Colin here fixed up with a good lawyer who can prove absolutely that he is the rightful chief of MacMhor.'

'I thought Rory inherited the title from his father?'

'He did, he did,' said Colin. 'But I don't suppose they've told you that our fathers were identical twins. And nobody really settled who was the elder. The old midwife took a heart attack and died soon after the birth. And the babies' mother died the following week. They were so alike Grandfather couldn't tell them apart and he decided it would be cosy — and convenient — if they shared the chieftainship.'

'What happened when they grew up then?'

'They were in the war and my father was killed a couple of days before Rory's. The fact is that my father never wanted to be chief of MacMhor. As soon as he could, he joined the regular army and left Uncle in full command.'

'Do you really want to be chief of MacMhor?'

'For only as long as it takes to sell Clodha to me,' said Felix with a guffaw.

'Shut up,' said Colin, his face flushed with anger. 'Surely you can see that everyone here would be better off if Felix bought it. Instead of the good old feudal days of Bannockburn, with cousin Rory seeing himself as a latterday Robert the Bruce, leading Scotland to freedom, we would be living in the twentieth century where we belong. There would be full employment for everyone.'

'Sure there would,' said Felix. 'With everything from an amusement park for the kiddies to a bingo hall for their parents. During the season we'd have Castle Clodha floodlit, of course. We wouldn't pull it down, it's too picturesque – if conversion to a hotel was too difficult we would gut the inside and leave the outside walls standing. Its atmosphere is just great, lends such a touch of class, the sort of thing American tourists go a bundle on.' He narrowed his eyes. 'And those cottages by the harbour, they could be turned into holiday chalets – I can see it all, can't you?'

I could and I shuddered, my sympathies with Rory and his cause, however lost or doomed.

'And, of course, Colin here, he would be rich, richer than he has ever dreamed. Made for life. I intend setting him up as manager of Clodha Holiday Island, in full control. Out of season, he could tinker with speedboats, and he'd never know what it was not to have the very best equipment money could buy. Maybe he would be famous some day . . .'

Gran appeared at the cottage door. 'May, don't sit there gossiping all day. It's time the hens were fed. Come away in, girl. And you, Colin MacMhor, always wasting someone's valuable time, I notice. How's your mother's new job?'

Studiously ignoring Felix Hall, Gran politely wished Colin good-day and shepherded me into the cottage. Closing the door, she said anxiously: 'So that daft man is back wanting Rory to sell him Clodha.'

'According to him it's just a social visit to Colin.'

Gran made an impatient gesture. 'Aye, but there'll be no making Rory MacMhor understand that.' Her face darkened. 'There'll be murder done on this island if Rory sets eyes on him. Colin MacMhor should have more sense. Wanting to sell our island to foreigners,' she added, totally ignoring that her grand-daughter fitted this category remarkably well. 'The English, always putting their noses where they shouldn't be.'

Hiding a smile, I put on the kettle for the hens' mash. Gran followed me into the kitchen. 'Mind you,' she said, 'we have some traitors, especially among the younger folk, influenced by the

American films and suchlike and the television, who think it might be a grand idea to have Clodha turned into a holiday camp.'

I shuddered. 'I think it would be sacrilege.'

'Do you now?' And she looked at me, I could have sworn, for the first time with approval. 'Sacrilege,' she repeated. 'Yes, indeed, and that is the very word. It is a great pity that Katrine does not marry Colin MacMhor and knock some sense into his daft ways, instead of that silly mother of his, with her city ways, encouraging his cars and his speedboats.' She sighed. 'He's a wild one, and no mistake, with a girl in every town across the water, so I'm told.'

'Perhaps Katrine isn't in love with him.'

Gran snorted. 'And what has being in love to do with marriage? In my day it was duty, not love, one married for. Duty to one's clan, to one's kin. The MacMhors' duty is to breed sons for Clodha,' she added sternly. 'And there is Katrine, getting older – in my day no man would have sought as his bride a woman of twenty-seven – but thank God she is still strong and healthy. 'Ah,' she sighed, 'when I think that her son could be the next chief of the MacMhor, if Rory does not marry. Perhaps he will not fly in the face of the Curse of Clodha again, for it has struck three times within living memory – so Katrine need not have any great hopes there.'

Nor need anyone else, whispered a small voice inside me, as I concluded that there was little Gran missed, for all her apparent withdrawal from active life.

'Reach me down that tin from the shelf,' she said, adding water to the bran. 'Ach, there I knew it. Tanoth's herbs are finished.' She shook her head. 'Katrine, Katrine – I do not know what is overcoming the girl, ever since she came back from Glasgow she has been a different person. It is as if some of their wild ways got into her. She used to be happy and content with Clodha, but since she returned there has been a restlessness – aye, more than that – as if two people wrestled inside my gentle Katrine.'

I said nothing, thinking only that the

solution to Katrine's problem could very speedily be solved by permanent residence at Castle Clodha, as the lady of the MacMhor.

'Ach, my poor hens,' Gran continued. 'It is grand herbs that Tanoth gathers, makes the creatures fairly lay – what eggs I get! Now I know why they have been poor and broody-like lately,' she shook the empty tin sadly, 'for Katrine will not go near Tanoth. She is afraid of her, thinks she is a witch. And most likely so, but her magic is white. Ach, well, well – and Tanoth is grand for all the island gossip. She'll be knowing about Colin and the foreigner and their plans.' The blue eyes that were so like my father's, but far shrewder, gave me a hard look. 'A pity now that you could not be driving Katrine's car . . .'

'I can't drive, but I would love the walk.'

'Well, now, that's fine then. You can be doing that after you've fed the hens.'

Mission accomplished in the hen-run, I wrote to Jim Scott, thanking him warmly for remembering me but assuring him that no repayment of his old debt to my

118

father was necessary. Then I answered Sarah's letter. 'You wouldn't believe it, but the whole setting yearns for a romantic novel. The island is beautiful but savage, the castle is haunted by the ghost of a murdered MacMhor mistress and the local Laird is a dish – unmarried too. I'm posting this on the way to the local witch (of the white variety) for a love-potion, believe it or not, for Gran's hens. Anything, it appears, can happen on Clodha. . . .'

On the way to Tanoth's cottage I realised what had eluded me about Colin. He and Rory were more alike than normal cousins because their father's had been identical twins. There was only one difference. Some unkind fate had given Colin the same features and colouring, but distributed to be almost a caricature of his cousin's. Colin's extrovert personality would be the one most remembered, but Rory, shy and sombre, could have rocked the world and left a trail of broken hearts from Land's End to John o'Groats had he inherited his cousin's easy charm.

As I climbed the cliff road, the sea far

below was bland and smooth, the black rocks sat in sunlight, like an army of basking seals.

Beyond the castle, seagulls danced in the sky, their echoing cries mingling with the oyster-catchers piercing 'peek ... peek ...' Perhaps there was a tractor planting out fields in the home farm, perhaps Rory himself was driving it. I pushed the thought aside. Whatever the crop, Rory MacMhor and Clodha would be long vanished from my life before its harvest.

Sunlight reduced Tanoth's cottage to reassuring normality, and pushing open the gate, I walked down the path with more courage than had marked my first encounter. The door was ajar and my hands trembled slightly as I remembered the strange interior.

What if she sat waiting for me in that huge chair? As she did on that first night, waiting to curse me again.

There was no reply to my timid knock, so I pushed open the door very cautiously and called: 'Miss MacMhor, are you there?'

Caught by a shaft of sunlight, pale

faces looked out at me, motionless, and I stepped back, once more caught off guard by the strange tapestry. Then I laughed at my ridiculous behaviour and as Tanoth was nowhere to be seen I decided to have a closer look. Even to my inexperienced eye the tapestry was obviously extremely old and its pattern quite worn away in places. But Tanoth, with clever fingers and her box of threads, was gradually breathing life into it again. There was the girl with red-gold hair, Rowan, whose ghost I had seen. Now, as I looked closer, I recognised another face – a man's.

My heart lurched as I recognised some ancestor of Rory MacMhor, for the face bore an uncanny resemblance to him and there was Castle Clodha in the background. As I leaned forward, for the sunlight had suddenly faded and the tapestry grew dim, I saw the turret window. Suddenly it was all very clear, somehow alive and menacing as it had been on that first night. I was aware of other faces, figures, shadows – peering out from behind trees, for at one time long past the spinney must have

121

extended for some distance down the hill. My eyes moved back to the turret window. There were no bars, but as I looked closer a woman's face appeared. Her hair was dark red . . .

Suddenly I jumped back in horror. As though I stared into a mirror, the face I saw was my own. . . .

I turned and ran from that poor and desolate room. At the door I paused, looked over my shoulder, with some idiotic idea that They might leap from the tapestry and follow me down the cliff road in swift but soundless pursuit, until finally enmeshed by Their ghostly arms, the air murmuring thick with Their angry whispers, I would be lifted and go hurtling through the air down into that hungry ever-waiting sea.

But there was nothing, nothing for me to fear. Sunlight filled the room and from the ancient faded tapestry pale faces watched, sad and featureless. Beside the bright St. Andrew's flag the only other living thing was the shining red-gold silk, the embroidered hair of Rowan, the witch of Clodha, who had appeared as if by magic out of the cruel rocks of Eilean na Gealach and with her beauty brought destruction to the wild MacMhors.

Chapter Eight

AS I hurried down the path from Tanoth's cottage, relieved to see another human being, a small boy who was being pulled up the cliff road by a very large and determined dog, shouted across: 'If you are wanting Tanoth, she will be away to the castle.'

An excuse, I thought, a glorious excuse to see Rory again. And – without interruption from Katrine.

I thanked the boy and said it was a fine day. However, he turned shy and the dog fairly hurled him along the road, where both disappeared in the direction of the home farm.

Still suffering from the effects of a tapestry that came alive in Tanoth's cottage, the feeling of being transported to a childhood fairy-tale mounted as I walked across the cobbled courtyard and knocked on the castle door. As I waited for someone to come, I looked around me, the sea, the harbour, the whitewashed cottages, minute birds moving in an azure sky. Fishing boats, a glimpse of blue far-off islands and, nearer, set in silver, the great ragged giant rocks of Eilean na Gealach – the Isle of the Moon.

I thought of my letter away to Sarah, of the boutique in Chelsea, soft lights, and pop music eternal in the background. I thought of London's great noisy heart beating twenty-four hours a day and away stretching its arms like a giant octopus, the lines of streets that marked its suburbs. Once, in one of those houses, each indistinguishable from its next-door neighbour, I had lived.

Impossible, it seemed, that soon I should return to a world still a hundred years away in time.

The castle door remained closed and, disappointed, I was about to leave when Tanoth MacMhor opened the door, wiping her hands of flour.

'Please—to—come—in. Welcome—welcome,' she added. So she did

understand English and could speak it if she wished, although it sounded rusty with little use.

I followed her into the great stone-flagged kitchen, where a fine smell of baking added a homely touch. I was delighted to observe that the electricity generator caged down the road had extended its purpose to include cooker and washing machine. Both looked new and I wondered if these were at the instigation of the rich girl from Perthshire, the MacMhor cousin to whom Rory had been engaged and who had so tragically died on Clodha. As I looked around there was much evidence of modernisation and hadn't Katrine said the fiancée was no great shakes at housework?

I indicated the empty tin of herbs, wondering if Tanoth would understand. She nodded vigorously and smiled. 'Wait—a—moment.'

There was nothing of the witch, white or otherwise, about Tanoth today. Seen in the light of Rory's modern kitchen, only the size and seating of the long well-scrubbed old table hinted that it also did service as a communal eating-place for the workers of the home farm. Tanoth, with her long pale hair pulled back into an elastic band, seemed small and innocent, a frown of concentration puckering a childish brow – a small girl let loose in Mummy's kitchen, to play at houses.

A door slammed. Behind us a footfall. The door opened and, without any need to turn round, my heart's erratic behaviour told me it was Rory who came in.

He took both my hands. 'May. What a welcome surprise,' and inclining his head: 'No Katrine today?' And I could have sworn he looked pleased when I said she had gone to Glasgow to visit her mother.

'So you will be on your own now.' He gave me a speculative glance. 'We will need to find a companion for you. When does Katrine return to Clodha?'

'She said a day or two.'

His smile widened. Oh, why did he have to smile just like that, melting my heart. He's Katrine's, not yours, that same heart murmured, protesting. How strange his eyes, black in anger, yet golden when he smiled, his long black eyelashes, like a woman's, the only softness in a face where cheekbones seemed to dominate, with bone structure a sculptor's dream, which time could not mar. His mouth and chin suggested strength and stubborness too, I suspected. Despite the Indian-straight black Clodha hair, so touchingly boyish in its unruliness, this was the face of a man I would rather have for a friend than a foe.

What was he saying? '... Then perhaps you will accept me as companion and let me look after you until Katrine returns ...'

I must be dreaming. No, I blinked and he was still there smiling, consulting his watch: 'Let me see. About seven o'clock. Will that suit you?'

He was escorting me, still wrapped in my dream of disbelief, to the door when the telephone rang. Tanoth looked at the kitchen extension her eyes wide with terror, as if it was something that might explode.

Rory smiled. 'Hold on, I'll answer it.' I

waited not sure what to do, watching his face with its changed expression, cold and angry. Even though the conversation was in Gaelic did not disguise that it was somehow very private. Finally, cupping his hand over the mouthpiece, he said: 'Sorry, May, this might take a little time. If you are in a hurry?'

I took the hint, smiled and said goodbye. But he was too preoccupied to notice me going, the last I heard a rapid-fire exchange of Gaelic in Tanoth's direction. With one frightened glance she bolted up the spiral staircase by which Katrine and I had first entered the long gallery and the Laird's study. Hugging to myself the joy that I would be seeing Rory that evening, I hardly noticed the cliff road until a red car hooted noisily and there was Colin at the wheel, with Felix at his side.

'What are you doing so far from home?' Colin asked. He shot a backward glance at the castle. 'You needn't answer if you don't want to, but you could only have been visiting my wicked cousin' — his eyes raked me over appreciatively — 'tch, tch, and quite unchaperoned too.

Hasn't anyone put you wise and told you about the wild, bad MacMhor men yet?'

'I was only looking for Tanoth for herbs for Gran's hens.'

His eyebrows raised mockingly. 'Is that a fact? Well, judging by your pretty blush you found more than you bargained for in Castle Clodha. Come on, tell us the truth, it was really love potions from Tanoth you were wanting?'

'Feel free to drop some in my tea any time, any day, Miss Lachlan,' said Felix Hall, with a leer.

'Now look what you've done, you've embarrassed the poor girl.' Colin opened the car door. 'Jump in and come with us?'

'Where to?' I asked suspiciously.

'Felix and I are trying out the speedboat. Oh come on, or are you a bad sailor?'

That challenge was too much. 'Of course not. I have always adored water, especially to sail on, anything from a pleasure steamer down the Thames to a fishing boat off the Kent coast.'

Colin indicated the door again. 'Prove it then,' he said.

'All right, I will.'

As I sat between them listening to Colin's bantering conversation, I decided he was a man one couldn't dislike. Shallow and a womaniser, maybe, a man I wouldn't trust an inch, but his flattery had wit and a kind of light-hearted charm, contrasting well with the clumsy overtures of gallantry from Felix Hall, whom great riches couldn't save from being a first-class bore.

'You don't have to be in love with a boy to enjoy his company,' Sarah had insisted in the past when I refused a casual date. How true, I thought, feeling flattered that Colin had sought me out, especially as he combined efficiency at the wheel of the speedboat with a certain elegance. Felix noticed it too and made a great deal of protest that Colin had promised him a shot of the wheel.

They switched over, Colin sitting with an arm casually around me, insisting that I must be feeling the cold. He fetched me a sweater from a locker and suddenly I looked up and Eilean na Gealach loomed dangerously near, dancing on the waves, as Felix waltzed the boat, laughing, showing off.

'Go easy,' said Colin, and put a hand on his arm. 'Go easy, Felix. You're approaching the graveyard of three-quarters of the fishermen of Clodha.'

'Stop worrying. I can tame anything, man, woman or machine,' said Felix. 'I just want a closer look so that I can decide where to fit your Moon Island into my holiday island scheme.'

At that moment the boat began to pitch fiercely, helpless as a cork in a maelstrom.

'You damned fool,' said Colin. 'You'll have us wrecked. Can't you see where we're going? And you told me you could navigate.'

Then I was sprawling in the bottom of the boat and we spun top-like in the fierce current, the engine helpless, spluttering in protest, powerless to deal with the tide. A second later Colin had pushed Felix aside and he joined me, white-faced now, in the bottom of the boat. When I had given up all hope, sure we would be dashed to pieces on the great rocks that loomed over our heads, the boat responded to Colin's expert handling and we were zooming out of danger, back to Clodha.

Felix grimaced, rubbing a bruised forehead, and standing up he darted furious looks at Eilean na Gealach now retreating, and cursed them with some fluency. 'I do hate to be beaten by a bunch of rocks. You should have let me get us out of there, Colin. Who the hell do you think you are, snatching the wheel, pushing me around?'

'Cut it out,' said Colin. 'You'll get no more shots of the wheel on my boat. You crazy fool, we were within seconds of being dashed to pieces – don't you realise we were staring death in the face?'

'Oh you Highlanders, you're so impossibly romantic. You dramatise everything – one or two waves . . .' Felix was very brave now, but I remembered his ashen face. He was still arguing with Colin when we neared the harbour and Colin, ignoring him, said to me:

'Like to try your hand at taking her in, May?'

'I'd love it.' And I suppose to the man standing on the headland, with a collie dog at his side, the scene took on more significance than was intended. Colin and I were both laughing, with his arms about me, guiding my hands on the wheel. I thought too late there was something familiar about the man on the shore. It was Rory. He must have seen us, but he turned on his heel abruptly and strode away, but not before I had observed, even at that distance, the cold rage on his face.

'That man – that was Rory MacMhor, wasn't it?' said Felix nervously.

Colin groaned. 'Now the fat's truly in the fire. He knows you're here on Clodha. Perhaps you'll get that meeting with him sooner than you expected,' he added grimly, helping me out of the boat.

On the quay I shivered. Cold suddenly, for a thin mist had stolen over the sun. Colin sniffed the air as he ushered me into the car. 'Aye, we're in for some bad weather, too. Sorry, May, you'll have to put away your bikini for a few days.' It was a silent journey up to Gran's and when I got out of the car and waved goodbye they both departed looking grim, Felix tense and scared despite his bravado. All around me the island was strangely silent, there was no birdsong, and the seagulls had vanished. Perhaps they felt murder in the air that day. . . .

Depression enveloped me and already as I dressed carefully, and made up my face to meet Rory that evening, I was certain I did so in vain. He would not come. I had committed the unforgivable and been seen with his enemy, Colin MacMhor. At seven-thirty prompt Gran yawned and went to bed. I switched on the radio and listened to pop music. Once I had loved it, now it jarred, because it didn't belong to Clodha.

When the old grandfather clock struck eight I told myself that it was fast and, of course, with the home farm and other matters to deal with, Rory MacMhor couldn't be expected to arrive on the dot. It wasn't as if he was keeping me waiting outside in the cold.

By eight-thirty, I was trying consolation. Why should he not come because of seeing me with Colin that afternoon? After all, Katrine was friendly with both men. 'Ah yes,' said conscience, 'but then Katrine has always lived here and you are merely a foreigner.'

By nine o'clock I had already made two time checks on the radio and found that the grandfather clock kept excellent time and by nine-thirty I was merely coldly furious at being stood up.

I looked out of the window for the hundredth time. Colin's prediction of rain was true. It streamed down the windows, lashed by a high gale. There were distressed noises issuing forth from the henhouse, so I decided to check that all was well before going off to bed. Damn Rory MacMhor, I told myself, trying desperately not to cry.

I was leaving the henhouse when I saw a dark shadow coming along the narrow lane which served as footpath from the harbour. His head was down against the rain, but Rory had to stop and speak, for I was boldly outlined against the light from the kitchen window.

In that light his face full of shadows looked grey, weary, his hair plastered down by rain was suddenly much older than his thirty years. At that moment all my anger vanished and I longed to put out my arms, take him in them and love him.

He looked at me grimly, as though it required some effort to remember who I was. 'Sorry about tonight. Perhaps some other time. I was delayed – unexpected. Good night.' He bowed and turning on his heel disappeared into the rain-streaked dusk.

I peered after him. He was carrying something wrapped under his arm, which he had tried to conceal as he talked.

How odd. Puzzled, I went into the house and was half-way up the stairs to the bedroom when I realised that what I had seen was the stock of a rifle, wrapped to protect it from the rain.

It was no surprise that shooting game would be a general occupation on Clodha. But at nine-thirty in the rain and dusk? And why the elaborate attempts that I shouldn't notice it? Was it because I might be angry that he had preferred to go shooting – surely not out of necessity to fill the pot – and broken our date?

As I lay wakeful the cold flood of

truth would no longer be ignored. The reason for the broken date, the concealed rifle – obviously Rory had no intention of coming to the cottage but had to say something when I appeared, for Rory MacMhor was after bigger game than rabbits that night, in the shape of Felix Hall.

The summer night is short in Scotland, there is little darkness. I thought I had not closed my eyes, but was haunted by Rory pursuing Felix through the dusk, up towards the spinney where the trees lay silent folded in sleep. I saw a girl's face at the barred turret window watching it all, pleased that another of the accursed MacMhors was doomed to die, this time by his own folly. I saw the rifle raised ... a shot ...

Suddenly I was wide awake sitting up in bed. I thought I screamed but it wasn't my voice I heard. The sound came from Gran's bedroom. I rushed in and she was sitting by the side of the bed moaning, her hands on her heart, at her feet on the floor, the shattered fragments of a glass.

She looked ill, queer, and as I gently

put her back into bed, she asked for her pills in a drawer on the dressing-table. In a few moments her breathing and colour were better and when I dashed downstairs for a cloth to mop up the spilled water and brought back another glass, she said:

'Did you say there were only three pills left? Och, that Katrine, going off to Glasgow and not remembering to check that I had plenty of the pills for my heart.'

'Don't worry, I'll get you some from the doctor in the morning. Sleep now, Gran.'

She shook her head. 'The doctor is over at Oban. We're healthy folk on Clodha,' she added proudly, 'so he comes across only once a week and holds a surgery in the village hall. And that was yesterday.'

'Do you have these attacks often?' I asked, thoroughly frightened.

The thin shoulders moved restlessly against the pillow. 'They vary. Sometimes two, three in a week, sometimes months between them.'

I tucked the clothes round her. 'Get

some rest, Gran. I'll go to Oban for your pills in the morning.'

She smiled. 'Aye, you could be doing that. There is not a great deal for you to do here on the island and the ferry waits for a couple of hours, so you can get a wee look at the shops.'

'Is there anyone who will stay with you while I'm away?' I said anxiously, for she still looked far from well.

'Tanoth will come. You can ask her on the way to the ferry.' She sat up. 'Ach now, I will have to write a note – not that she can read more than the simplest words. It is a pity you do not have the Gaelic, child – it was most remiss of your father not to teach you,' she added severely. 'Go you to bed now and get some sleep.'

Downstairs the clock struck five. I knew there was no sleep for me. 'I'll stay with you for a while.'

She smiled and seemed pleased, rather shyly taking my hand in her thin frail one. On an impulse I leaned over and kissed her cheek. This time she didn't pull away, but patted my hand with a sigh: 'You're a grand bairn really – just like my wee laddie was.' And suddenly she was telling me about him, his childhood on the island and I could see through her eyes, fishing at the harbour, his first pony, his first boat. 'A good scholar, too, he was, if his father had been alive he might have gone to the university in Glasgow ...'

Taking her breakfast upstairs an hour later, I felt a new closeness, a new understanding. I prepared the hen's mash, but in the henhouse found a very scared flock. Murder had been done. Two pullets were dead and by the amount of terror and feathers in evidence, more had narrowly escaped.

Gran took the news calmly. 'That will be the rats again. I'll ask Sandy Lachlan when he comes with the post to spread some poison, there's a tin in the shed.'

An hour later I was on my way to Tanoth's cottage, resolutely determined not to let my eyes linger on Castle Clodha with sentimental dreams about Rory MacMhor, dreams I knew could never come true. After all, what did it matter to me what befell him — as far as he was concerned I was only a holiday curiosity, a visitor to his island and some ancient chivalry dictated he should treat with hospitality even the hated Sassenach within his gates. That was all the broken date meant to him. ...

There was nothing sinister about the cottage today, or the small figure busy cleaning the windows on a step ladder. From the distance Tanoth looked like a child. When I gave her Gran's note she thrust the bucket and mop into the room with the tapestry, seized a large shopping bag and pulled on a cardigan. As we walked down the road, she took my hand, and gave me a shy smile, like a gentle trusting child, but when I tried to make conversation she shook her head and laughed as if she didn't understand a word. The idea was quite ridiculous, but her presence made me strangely happy. I felt protected too and I wondered if she remembered our first encounter. Could this be the same woman who had warned me and Katrine had translated that warning as: 'Evil comes—danger— death— you will die on Clodha'?

Even in the sunlight I shuddered. The words seemed indelibly printed on the bright sea far below. There was only a little time left for that prophecy to be fulfilled, I thought, watching a small cloud drift over the island, moving swiftly, darkening the green. Nothing could move it backwards on its course, it progressed nearer towards us like the inevitable hand of Fate.

At the harbour our ways parted and Tanoth took both my hands in hers, clasping them tightly palms together, as though I prayed. She raised her eyes above my head, back up the hill to rest I knew on Castle Clodha.

Then she bowed her head and I began to tremble, sick at heart. What new terror lay ahead this time?

Suddenly her head jerked upwards, she looked into my eyes and smiled:

'So May has come at last? We have been waiting for you. Why did you take so long? So long . . . so long . . .'

She released my hands and sped away along the road to Gran's cottage. Beside me, the ferry honked its warning. In a daze I went aboard, Tanoth's words echoing in my head. For they were said in perfect English and it was not the first time I had heard them either. The first time was from a dream – or was it? – of a girl with red-gold hair, the witch of Clodha, whom I had seen as I waited sleepily for Katrine to return in the Laird's study in Castle Clodha.

Chapter Nine

FROM the almost empty ferry Clodha was a blurred picture of washed-out greens and greys under an overcast sky, the sea calm and colourless. Even the harbour was unusually deserted, Colin MacMhor's fishing fleet presumably storm-bound beyond Eilean na Gealach and his precious speedboat tucked safely away in its boathouse.

The ferry had just cast off when a figure raced down the quay and jumped on board. It was Rory. I felt the colour rise to my cheeks and confused, sure that all my secret longings lay blatantly across my face for any man to read, I fled into the passengers' cabin.

Rory hadn't seen me and, leaning on the rail, he scanned the sea, eyes narrowed intently. A man who searches ... watched this new and secret face, pleased that he couldn't see me. But not for long. With the instinct that tells someone they are under surveillance, he turned, searching for the prying eyes and found mine.

He came down the steps into the cabin and smiled politely across the line of seats.

'Good morning, May,' he said with a small bow and moving swiftly to the starboard side resumed his watch over the sea.

I was furious. Not content with breaking our date last night, his intention was apparently to ignore me all the way to Oban. The realisation that, preoccupied and remote, he looked more handsome, more inaccessible than ever, did nothing to charm me out of my bad humour. It was too much. I marched past him and back on to the deck.

A few moments later I was gratified by his voice asking: 'Going to Oban?'

'Why? Do I have a choice?' I replied

coldly, but sarcasm was lost on him.

'I suppose I owe you an apology for last night,' he said, sounding amused and not in the least contrite.

'You suppose right.'

'Come now, May, don't be angry, yours is too pretty a face to spoil with that petulant look. I'm sorry, but something urgent came in the way.'

I swung round angrily. 'That apology would have been kinder at seven than at nine-thirty last night. And our meeting then, I gather, was purely accidental.'

As though suddenly bored with me, he shrugged and leaning on the rail, he resumed his watch over the sea, eyes now black and intent, face impassive. 'All right, be angry. You are entitled to it – enjoy your wrath, May Lachlan.'

'I am not enjoying my wrath.'

'The situation was difficult and delicate. I didn't know how to explain to a nicely brought-up Sassenach ...'

He managed to make the word an insult. 'Oh, you ...' and my raised hand as I sought for a sufficiently insulting word was a purely reflex action. My wrist was caught mid-air in a vice-like grip.

'Do not be thinking to strike me, May Lachlan. I warn you, I could not forgive that, even from you,' he said, in the soft dangerous tones I recognised from our first encounter on Clodha when I had mistaken him for the estate factor. I looked up into his face, eyes secret, the straight lines of a mouth tightened in anger that could be cruel and frightening too.

'I had no intention of being so uncouth,' I said coldly, as he released my wrist. 'I leave such barbarities to my kin on Clodha.'

But Rory wasn't listening, his eyes still searching my face. 'Would you know,' he asked gently, 'how to tell someone – a girl – that you could not meet her because that night you might – have to kill a man?'

'Kill a man.' The words hung matter-of-fact on the air. He uttered them in the same fashion as Gran had said when her hens were attacked: 'Kill the rats.'

My emotions must have shown clearly, for he smiled mockingly. 'It's all right, you don't need to bound away to safety like a scared gazelle. I did not find Felix Hall. Luckily – he and my cousin Colin had hopped over to Oban.'

'Is that – why you are here? Is that what you're doing – following them?'

Rory shrugged. 'That will depend entirely on what my lawyer has to say. You know, I gather, from your couthy afternoon in Colin's speedboat, that he wants to sell Clodha to Hall. For a holiday camp. The only way to do so is over ´my dead body, or, if I remain obstinately alive, by proving he is the rightful chief of MacMhor – in fact, that his father was the elder twin.' He paused. 'Not that his chieftainship would glorify him or benefit Clodha – he only wants it long enough to sell Clodha to Felix Hall.'

And Felix Hall had told me so in as many words. I felt sympathy for Rory's anger.

'You can't kill a man because he wants to buy Clodha.'

'Can I not now?' he asked softly, the dark eyebrows raised.

'We will see about that. To save Clodha from the fate of a Halcyon Holiday Camp, even the prospect of murder does not appal me. My patriotism goes deep, make no mistake about that, May Lachlan. In such a position I would be merely a soldier defending his land, where murder is called killing the enemy.' He looked at me slowly. 'So I've shocked you, have I? That is too bad, but Clodha is *my* country. My land, as dear to me as life itself. And I will not sit aside and watch her degraded, ravished, ruined by funfairs and casinos and bingo halls. In the old clan warfare days, we often killed our women to save them falling into the hands of the enemy. In the same way I would destroy Clodha to save her shame.' He was silent for a moment watching Eilean na Gealach with its cruel rocks like the craters of the moon draw nearer.

'You see, May, I *am* Clodha. Her life is mine and her death my death.'

A bleak sunshine wavered over the sea, touched briefly the stony profile of this alien man that I loved.

Yes, I was in love now for the first time. With this creature from another world. From Clodha, *his* Clodha, with its colourful pageant of witches, curses, family feuds, all jogging along by the side of the twentieth century, but never part of it.

At that moment I was as gratified by the discovery of my love for Rory MacMhor as if I had fallen in love with a visitor from Mars. Either would have been equally unenviable as a romantic prospect.

I was greatly relieved to notice as we reached the harbour at Oban that there was no sign of Colin's speedboat, though my companion, if such a word could be used to describe the silent man at my side, appeared to be distinctly disappointed. As we walked down the gangway he said: 'After this somewhat revealing journey I would hesitate to ask you to have lunch with a monster. Besides, who knows what Fate holds in store for a pretty girl on her own in Oban for the day.'

Without a word, I turned and walked away from that mocking face. My temper, cooled by the time I had collected Gran's pills, was further consoled by a handsome cashmere sweater and matching skirt, bought in one of Oban's beautiful knitwear shops. I was beginning to enjoy myself, with prospects of exploring, but as I lingered over coffee, the warm sea breeze turned into a coldish wind with flurries of rain.

If the weather was changing then I had better get back to Clodha as soon as possible and I hurried down to the ferry to find a chain across the gangway.

'Not today, lass,' said the pilot, with a look at the darkening sky. 'Not this morning, anyway. We would never make it, not with the tide from Eilean na Gealach boiling like a witch's cauldron.'

'Then how will I get back?'

He gave me a pitying glance. 'You will just have to be making the best of it, as the island folk do. And be thinking yourself lucky. Aye, last night a man was drowned off a yacht just beyond the bar over there. The coastguard's launch is still out looking for him, or his corpse, and there seems little to doubt which they will be finding.' He shook his head. 'Ach, these foreigners, they will not be taking a telling.'

'And someone should have told you

the importance of never leaving Clodha without an overnight case,' said Rory's mocking voice at my elbow.

'But what shall I do?' And forgetting my fury with him, I told him about Gran's pills.

'If she only takes one of these pills at each attack, then it is unlikely that she will need three before you return, especially as you say she was a little better before you left. Besides, she is in good hands, never fear, with Tanoth. And let me tell you, Tanoth has many a herb up her sleeve for an emergency ...'

'That's all very well ...'

'Of course it is.' He took my elbow and steered me back on to the quay. 'There is absolutely no point in you worrying. Your gran will come to no harm. So how about having lunch with me, after all, just to fill in a little while before the storm calms down again. Don't worry, you'll get back to Clodha in a few hours ...'

Determinedly I began to walk away from him. 'Please don't bother to be polite. I'm sure there are lots of things you have to do on Oban. There is absolutely no need to feel responsibility for entertaining me ...'

He seized my arm, and jerked me to a standstill. In the same quiet voice he had used on the ferry he said: 'I do not feel the slightest responsibility for you and I am not in the habit of being polite to anyone, unless I wish to be. You have the offer, May Lachlan. Take it or leave it, as you wish. I really don't care one way or the other.'

The rain was heavy now, a steady downpour and we must have looked an odd sight standing there arguing. A set-piece in a one-act drama.

'Mr. MacMhor – sir!'

A taxi stopped alongside us. 'Jump in, sir,' said the driver, 'and I'll be taking you up to the hotel.'

Rory looked at me and smiled. 'Yes or no? You might as well be warm and comfortable with a good meal inside you while we wait. Come along, May.' As the driver bowed us into the car, cap in hand, I noticed, despite the rain, and closed the door on us, Rory said: 'They have an excellent supply of magazines at the hotel. There will not be the slightest need for us to talk to each other at all.'

And I sat back well into my corner of the seat, wishing I had something for my injured dignity to brood over, but aware only of a steady tide of warm content.

. . .

One thing I had not bargained for was that Roderick Malcolm MacMhor, chief of MacMhor, might be such an important person away from the Isle of Clodha. I certainly had not bargained for the feudal splendour of his reception at the enormous Victorian hotel where manager, under-manager and head waiter all lined up to shake him by the hand in reception. Moments later we were being escorted across a deep pile carpet into a huge lounge, where heavy tartan furnishings and stags' heads were compensated by a cheerful log fire crackling away in a massive stone fireplace.

'Your shoes are damp. Take them off,' said Rory. And as I sat gratefully warming stockinged feet at the fire, he ordered drinks. 'I am having whisky, what will yours be?'

'Whisky, too, please,' I said, hoping to

sound casually sophisticated and ignoring a well-known incapacity to deal with spirits.

It came and I sipped it carefully. Even with a lot of water which Rory added rather contemptuously, I thought, it still burned my mouth. Rory finished his, ordered another, picked up the daily paper, read it silently and the waiter came in to guide us into lunch.

Scotch broth, Angus steak and trifle. And the damage begun by whisky was heightened by wine and completed by the warm lounge fire, whence we returned with our coffee.

In no time at all I was telling Rory the story of my life. Sarah's boutique, Dad's death and even brought bang up to date with the mysterious letter I had received, forwarded to Clodha by Sarah, from Dad's friend, Mr. Scott.

'Katrine thinks I might be an heiress,' I said, and realised this was the first time Katrine's name had been mentioned. I was immediately sober, made sober by my guilty feelings.

'Do you like her?' I asked recklessly.

'Who? Oh, Katrine. Of course.' He

seemed surprised. 'My dear girl, we've been friends since childhood. I used to regularly fish her out of the sea and teach her how to climb rocks. I helped her sail her first boat – one made of paper. She was the first girl I ever summoned up enough courage to kiss. She was eight, I think, and I was twelve.'

'Are you going to marry her?' How arch I sounded, nobody would have guessed that I cared about the answer to that one.

'Because of that first kiss? Don't you think that's rather a severe penalty?' Then suddenly he wasn't laughing any more, but staring into the burning logs. 'Do you think I should marry Katrine Lachlan? Perhaps she would make me a good wife?' I said nothing. 'Do I take your silence to mean no, then?'

I was sitting on the hearth-stool at his feet, leaning against his chair. Above my head I heard him laugh. 'My wee lamb – are you still awake? Yes? I think I have made you rather drunk. At least if you must sit away down there, rest your head on my knee ...'

Furiously, I sat up. 'I will not. I'd feel

like Shep.'

'And what, may I ask, is wrong with Shep? A fine old dog, a trusting and faithful companion?' Gently he turned me round to face him.

'Well, I don't want to be your trusting and faithful companion,' I said indignantly, pulling away from him.

Suddenly my face was in his none-too-gentle hands, the storm-dark eyes, golden now, mere inches away. 'And what *do* you want to be, then?' he whispered.

The necessity of an embarrassing reply in my reckless condition was saved by a page calling: 'Telephone for Mr. MacMhor.'

My face hectically flushed, I went over to the rain-washed windows. The storm had worsened. In the garden the tree-tops danced crazily, their leaves turned inside out by the wind. I laid my burning face against the cool window-pane.

Rory came back from the telephone, ordered another whisky and said: 'Sorry, May. We're stranded in Oban until the storm dies down. The gale warning is out and there won't be a ferry back to Clodha today.'

'But what about Gran? And where shall I stay?'

'First things first,' said Rory. 'This isn't the end of the world. Mrs. Lachlan won't worry, she knows the treacherous seas all too well. In a similar situation – many, many times a year it happens, it isn't just to spite you – Katrine usually stays with some Lachlans who run a boarding house down the road. Hold on . . .' He took out a notebook. 'I have the phone number – here.'

I went through to reception and dialled the number. But the Lachlans were full up. As they said apologetically, it was a popular time, early summer, for the overseas tourists and did I not know that there was an English Convention in Oban that week? They were sorry, but there would not be a room to be had in Oban. After the fourth call in vain I concluded they were right and reported the situation to Rory. 'Where will you stay?' I asked him.

'Here. My great-great-grandparents owned this place in happier days. It was built for them, and while the castle was being modernised they found it useful, especially in winter when Clodha was cut off from the mainland for long periods. At that time they owned very much more land hereabouts and it was convenient to have a house on the mainland. So we still own a small suite of rooms which comes in useful occasionally. Don't worry – I'm sure there'll be a spare room somewhere in the hotel for you.'

Very soon after that we lost the cosiness of having a pleasant lounge all to ourselves and discovered that the hotel too was full of members of the Midlands Convention who arrived back from their day's outing in time for dinner.

Rory did not seem pleased by this turn of events and after disappearing to talk to the manager he came back and said: 'Sorry, May, not a hope of a single room for you, I'm afraid. They're already overcrowded. They'll see if they can find a camp-bed, that's the best they can do.'

'Excuse me, sir,' said the head waiter. 'Do you wish dinner in the dining-room or shall we serve it in your suite?'

Rory looked around the crowded settees and chairs. 'The suite, I think,

Robert, would make a splendid retreat from your English invasion.'

'Very good, sir. Whenever you are ready. There has been a fire going for sometime, as you instructed.'

'Thank you, Robert.' And Rory led me up the great red-carpeted stair on to the first floor where the MacMhor suite overlooked the harbour. A bright fire burned in the hearth, and thick red plush curtains were drawn shutting out the wind and rain. The sitting-room was furnished in the rather ebullient manner of a century ago and I suspected its contents would be very valuable as antiques. It managed to achieve the right note of grace, charm and comfortable luxury too. A room to linger in, to enjoy.

'It's absolutely beautiful,' I said.

'Come and see the rest of it.' Rory opened the door into a large bedroom with a brass plaque set into the mantelpiece saying that Queen Victoria and Prince Albert occupied these rooms as guests of the MacMhor on their Highland visits. Another door led into a smaller bedroom, neat and attractive with its single brass bed and rosewood furniture. On the marble-topped chest was a floral china ewer and bowl.

'That belongs to the days before my grandfather had the bathroom over there' – Rory indicated a door alongside – 'installed. These two smaller rooms were for the lady's maid and the Laird's body-servant who accompanied them everywhere.'

Behind us the door opened and dinner was wheeled in under silver covers, the table pulled forward in front of the fire. Then the evening began to vanish, as we ate and sipped our wine, the last of our precious day together slipped away like sand through an hour-glass. For three hours we talked, sometimes with laughter, sometimes with fierce argument, for the things I learned about Clodha and the MacMhors' still feudal rights horrified my twentieth-century mind.

'That's only because you're a product of the welfare state,' Rory said. 'I can assure you that the islanders are very happy to leave all decisions to the MacMhors.'

'And what about the idea of turning it

into a holiday camp? I understand some of the younger members of the community were enthusiastic. Did you ever consider taking a democratic vote on the subject?'

That was too much for Rory, who angrily demanded how could they decide what was best for them and proceeded to deliver a lecture on the terrible consequences of such a plan and if it failed how it could result in complete depopulation of yet another island. From this starting-point he launched into his dream — of a Scotland free from English domination. And listening to his arguments, even with my lack of political understanding or interest, I began to see quite unwillingly the whole tide of English-Scottish politics since the days of Edward Longshanks and Robert the Bruce as a brutal series of injustices.

I realised something else. Until I came to Clodha, like most of the southern English, I regarded Scotland not as a separate country but as part of England, vaguely north of Northumberland, intensely cold in climate, where the men wore kilts and ate porridge. I had tolerated my father's stubborn attitude of intense loyalty about Scotland and Clodha, especially as he would never return to the land of his birth, as vaguely amusing, the rather colourful romanticism of middle age. Now I saw that resentment of England had real cause and although I could not agree with every part of Rory's argument, one fact emerged: the Scots had great pride in race, too much pride to tolerate for ever their position as a province of England.

'Now do you realise,' said Rory, 'that there are men and women who would give their lives to see Scotland free?'

'Like you?'

He nodded slowly. 'Like me. My responsibility to Clodha is just part of the greater issue, my dislike of Felix Hall part of a darker tide of tyranny, of a yoke we have smarted under these past centuries.'

'And do you think killing one man, like Hall, would cure Clodha's wistful dreams of sliding into the twentieth century with a few of the amenities quite normal people who aren't ogres, enjoy such as television?'

'It is my greatest wish that Clodha should prosper, that my people be happy – with television and cinema and whatever. But the means of obtaining such amenities, as you call them, must not be through the hopelessly corrupt influence of men like Felix Hall.'

'If you destroy him, another ten will only take his place . . .'

Rory laughed. 'Please – May. I was exaggerating, you know. At least I found out today that whether or not my uncle Colin's father was the elder twin, he renounced all rights to be chief of the MacMhor before leaving Clodha to join the British Army' – and he managed to make it sound foreign too – 'so Colin and Hall simply haven't got a case. As long as I live Clodha is mine and only if I die without a son will Colin have his way.'

'Doubtless you will marry.'

'Doubtless.' He shrugged. 'To be honest, although it is my duty for the sake of the MacMhors and for Clodha, I have little real inclination for marriage. Or maybe I haven't met the woman who has changed my mind. As you've probably gathered, I'm a solitary person by nature and habit.' He paused and then added lightly, toying with his wineglass, 'Wouldn't the curse of Clodha dampen any girl's interest in me as a prospective husband?'

Carefully I avoided his eyes. 'Do you believe in it?'

'The evidence is all around you on Clodha, isn't it? And as you probably know, my fiancée died – violently.' He looked at the clock. 'Well, May, I still have some writing to do and it's well past midnight. Time you were off to bed, anyway. Good heavens, I wonder if they found a place for you. Hold on, I'll just ring downstairs,' and he disappeared into the bedroom.

A few moments later he returned. 'Sorry, May, the whole establishment closed down at midnight, only the night porter on duty. I'm afraid there's nothing for it but the spare bedroom here – if you don't mind.'

'Of course not. That'll be fine.'

He opened the door for me. 'It seems right and fitting that you should sleep here, May Lachlan. After all, it was always occupied by a Lachlan in the old days when Lachlan was the hereditary piper and body-servant of the MacMhor.' He handed me the key.

'I don't need that.'

He bowed. 'Very kind of you. But as neither your grandmother nor Queen Victoria would be amused by such an unseemly lack of convention, I think you had better lock your door.'

'What nonsense. I trust you.'

He leaned towards me and suddenly without warning I was gathered into his arms. He kissed me once, twice. The moment seemed endless. Then he released me: 'My dear innocent child,' he whispered, 'thank you for trusting me, but you see how it is. I don't trust myself – so for my sake, lock your door.'

With that the bedroom door closed and I was on the other side of it. 'Good night, sleep well,' he called.

Chapter Ten

WITH more reason than the strange bed, I dozed fitfully, hearing Rory moving about in the next room, and the first faint movements of life stirring in the hotel and a dawn full of birdsong. At last I slept apparently only for minutes, to be awakened by a maid bringing in tea.

When I went through to the sitting-room later, Rory was already seated at the writing-desk.

'Good morning,' he smiled. 'I trust you slept well. Good — there's breakfast over there — yes, I've had mine.'

Cup in hand, I wandered across to the window, where sunlight flooded a silver sea, like a great mirror shining across towards Clodha.

'Come along,' said Rory, 'do eat something.' He indicated the silver-covered dishes on the trolley. 'Bacon, eggs, porridge . . .'

'No, thank you. I never eat breakfast, honestly'. And I went back to staring down into Oban. Suddenly I was aware of him standing behind me.

'Is there something wrong?' he asked.

'Of course not.'

'You aren't generally silent for such a long time. Sure?'

'I was just thinking yesterday was such a lovely day, despite the rain and everything.' That was quite an understatement. Yesterday had been the happiest day in my whole life, one day I would never forget. The sun hadn't shone, the wind had blown a hurricane and the rain had lashed a wild sea. But for me it was a day out of paradise, because I had spent it almost entirely with this man I loved.

'I hope you weren't bored. There isn't much entertainment in the rain . . .'

'Oh, I loved just talking to you – it was wonderful.'

He took my hands. 'Was it, May Lachlan? I'm so glad.'

I thought he was going to kiss me again, but he released my hands and went back to his writing-desk, gathering papers together. There's a fellow taking me back to Clodha in his rowing boat. Saves waiting for the ferry . . .'

Saves our faces, too, I thought. No doubt there would be plenty of speculation when Rory MacMhor returned with me after spending the night in Oban.

'You haven't forgotten that Katrine will be back this morning.' I had. 'You might as well explore Oban and go back with her on the ferry. Don't look so crushed, little one,' he said, and took my face between his hands. 'It's better this way,' he added quietly. 'In your own words we had a wonderful day, but that was yesterday. Today and tomorrow, I'm afraid, will be a lot different.'

Abruptly he began to thrust papers into his briefcase. 'You have some time left on Clodha, I know, but I'm not intending seeing more of you than I can possibly help. Quite frankly, I realised after last night, it's better this way.'

'What do you mean − after last night? Nothing happened last night.'

He smiled. 'Nothing to you, maybe, but to me it was something of a revelation. I didn't sleep very well, May Lachlan, thanks to your presence just a wall away, and I spent a considerable part of the wakeful hours dreaming about what *could* have happened. Look,

I don't want to hurt you, so surely you see it's kinder to keep out of your way.'

I said nothing.

'Isn't it – kinder?' he insisted.

'Don't you think perhaps keeping out of my way is the best way to hurt me?'

He seized me by the shoulders. 'I'm a man, May Lachlan. And I want you – very much. You still don't understand, do you? My heart's darling,' he whispered, 'I'm a little in love with you, I think. You're young and sweet and very pretty. You're gentle and trusting and by no means what I expected a London girl to be.' He shook me gently. 'You see, there are many reasons why I must send you away before you end up as the next candidate for the curse of Clodha.'

I put my arms around his neck. 'Oh, Rory, I'm so glad.'

'Don't be a little fool,' he said roughly.

'I don't care about the MacMhors, cursed and wild as they may be. Honestly I don't, I'll take a chance on that. I only care that I love you. I love you, Roderick Malcolm MacMhor.'

He smiled and said: 'I believe you do, you silly girl. But remember when you're sane again that love isn't all. Think how you, a city girl, would cope with Clodha, how would you survive the isolation, the loneliness, to say nothing of the responsibilities of being my wife. You have to be born to it. Would even your love survive? – you know how we'd argue, as we did last night. There are so many things you'd hate about me, about my life – my feudal kingdom, as you called it. Don't say we wouldn't quarrel – yes, we would – every time we've met so far, remember, we've ended up by fighting . . .'

I kissed him, obliterating the rest of the words. 'Do stop protesting, Rory MacMhor. Love can conquer all things . . .'

But a moment later he was free, pacing the room again. 'Go away, May,' he said thickly. 'I'm not getting involved . . .'

He was interrupted by a tap on the door. 'That will be the man with the boat, waiting for me,' he said with too obvious relief, and, taking up raincoat and briefcase, he said: 'Goodbye, May. No, I'm not going to argue – or to kiss you again. This is goodbye.'

Ten minutes later I left the hotel and walked around Oban in a daze. The sunshine, the beauty of the day, meant nothing to me. My wildest dreams had come true and had turned to ashes. Yesterday, if I had considered that Rory should even kiss me, joy would have been boundless. Today he had kissed me, he had told me he loved me. But we were further away from each other than ever.

Katrine was very surprised to see me on the ferry, but only concerned with relating her own adventures. How happy she was that she and her mother had got along so splendidly together on this Glasgow jaunt – to the extent of Katrine being bought a new suitcase full of bright and trendy clothes. She presumed I had come for Gran's pills on the first ferry from Clodha that morning.

No need to enlighten her, or spoil her happiness by casting the shadow of Rory MacMhor between us. She'll find out soon enough, I thought grimly.

'What have you been doing with yourself, May? Seen anything of Rory?' She took my non-committal 'Well . . .' as a negative and laughed. 'He's always too busy for anything. Going up to the castle this afternoon will have to be my very first job,' she sighed. 'Really, the man's so helpless, there'll be plenty for me to do.' She laughed happily. 'You must tell me what I shall wear from my new wardrobe. Blue's his favourite colour and I'm always greatly missed when I've been out of his sight for a day or two ... Oh, look. There's Colin with the boat. Come on ...'

We ran along the quay to where Colin was starting his speedboat. 'You didn't need to come all this way for me,' said Katrine, jumping aboard, 'Colin dear, I could have taken the ferry.'

'A pleasure, my darling,' said Colin, kissing her fondly. And as he helped me into the boat, there was a knowing glint in his eyes. 'And *how* is May Lachlan this bright and sunny morning?'

Mercifully, Katrine's, 'And how is Felix Hall?' saved me answering his question.

'Haven't the faintest idea,' said Colin grimly. 'After we left you the other afternoon, May, we came across to

Oban. Felix said he wanted to look around and intended taking the ferry back to Clodha yesterday morning. When he didn't arrive I presumed the storm had delayed him. However, he didn't turn up for our appointment with the lawyer. I've asked in various places, but nobody's seen him.'

'Where on earth can he be?' asked Katrine.

'Know what I think?' said Colin, his eyes on distant Clodha. 'I think he came back all right and found my cousin Rory waiting for him. With a shotgun. And that was that,' he said significantly.

My heart racing, I said: 'Can you prove it?'

He studied me slowly, rather insolently. 'I can prove plenty of people saw Rory wandering about Clodha with a rifle two nights ago.'

And, sickened, I remembered too. How I had been afraid of the tense, sleep-walking expression in his eyes when I met him. Even loving him, I had thought him capable of murder. Then yesterday, his wild talk about killing Felix Hall, about Scotland's freedom —

173

as a soldier destroys the enemy for his country.

How could my love for Rory survive such a blow? Now the wisdom of his words in the hotel this morning came back to me. How could I ever adjust my moral training to live with a race of men who took such violence without the slightest qualm?

He was waiting for us on the quay. For me, for Colin, for Katrine — which?

'Hello, Rory,' said Katrine, uncomfortable at being confronted in Colin's presence.

'Hello, had you a good time in Glasgow?' And helping me out of the boat: 'I find you keeping strange company, May Lachlan,' and the mockery in his eyes was dimmed by another emotion — anger.

'Here, cousin Rory. Not so fast.' And Colin, laughing, yelled something after him in Gaelic. Rory dropped my arm and turning launched himself on his cousin.

Both men were of a height and well matched for weight, but my every instinct was still to rush forward and separate them.

Katrine grabbed my arm. 'Keep out of this, May. It's none of your business.'

'None of my business! They'll kill each other. We must do something – for heaven's sake, Katrine.'

'Do something – about what?' And Katrine laughed. 'This happens regularly. One of the sights of Clodha. People come from far and near to see the wild MacMhors at each other's throats. It happens every time they meet face to face. Colin insults Rory or Rory insults Colin and then they're both obliged to do battle with each other.' She paused. 'I wonder what girl Colin was referring to?'

Anxiously I watched the struggling figures, disgustedly the small audience that had crept down from everywhere to enjoy the spectacle of a good fight. And I felt shame and sorrow for a place where passions lay so primitively close to the surface and sudden revulsion for the fighters, rolling so undignifiedly about the ground in front of me. Sick at heart, if a magic carpet could have transported me away from Clodha never to return I would have been back in London that instant.

Katrine clasped my arm. 'I wonder who she was?'

'Who?' I said absently, nervously intent on following Rory's swinging fists now that both men were on their feet again.

'The girl Colin accused Rory of spending the night with in Oban.'

I looked at her. How on earth did Colin know?

There was a yell from Colin. Rory had his arm twisted in a wrestler's hold. 'He'll break his arm,' I said. 'Do something.'

Katrine laughed. 'Don't be daft. This is the way it always ends. Look, I told you.' And Rory flung his cousin aside. He dusted down his clothes with great dignity and as Katrine ran to Colin's side, Rory grabbed my arm and marched me firmly past the gaping, whispering faces, up the road to Gran's cottage.

Once I looked back. Katrine was following us, Colin having presumably departed in the direction of his garage.

'Let's wait for Katrine,' I panted, but Rory never slackened his murderous pace.

Breathlessly she caught up with us and a strange silent trio we made, marching up the hill as if all the king's horses and all the king's men were at our heels. Rory looked neither left nor right and resisted all attempts at conversation when we had breath to spare for remarks. But he held on to my arm in a vice-like grip, as if for some reason he thought I might escape.

Gran, placidly knitting at her door, was a strangely peaceful contrast to the scene we had left at the harbour.

She looked at Rory's bruised cheekbone. 'Aye, so you and that daft laddie your cousin have been fighting again. You never learn, do you, Rory MacMhor. You'll both be fighting to the day the Lord takes you home.'

Rory didn't answer but, opening the gate, thrust me before her like a truant child captured out of school.

'I have something to say to you, Mrs. Lachlan. I believe you are May Lachlan's only relative.'

'I am that.'

He bowed stiffly. 'Then that is well. I wish you to know that I intend having your grand-daughter in marriage.'

Bowing to her, he turned on his heel and began striding up the hill to the castle. I turned to Gran, started to explain, heard the strangled cry from Katrine's white face, saw the look of utter amazement on Gran's and rushed after Rory.

I seized his arm. 'Rory. Rory, please stop. We must talk about this.'

He stopped and looked down at me, eyes black with anger, the bruise on his cheek, where Colin had struck him, darkening already. 'What have we to say, May Lachlan? You said you loved me and when I warned you that the MacMhors were doomed you said you didn't care. That was only a few hours ago. Are you telling me you have changed your mind already?' he asked icily.

'If you treat me like this – like cattle to be bought – I certainly have changed my mind. You might at least have done the courtesy of asking me to marry you before making a public announcement of it.'

'I did not make a public

announcement,' Rory said flatly, 'merely made my intentions clear to your grandmother, in case there was any misunderstanding. However archaic such actions seems to you, a foreigner, this happens to be the custom on Clodha.'

'You might also add that it was purely in defence of Colin's accusation, because you were furious with him.'

'You were not named personally . . .'

'Then don't presume to make an honest woman of me, Rory MacMhor. I am quite capable of looking after myself and my own reputation without any help from you. You needn't add me to your collection of responsibilities on Clodha out of any misguided sense of duty.'

'Then you wish to be released . . .?'

'I do indeed.'

'Be it as you wish,' he said coldly, and turning our backs on each other we walked away after the shortest betrothal in Clodha's history. Yesterday it was beyond my wildest dreams that Rory could be my husband. Within a few hours we had loved, exchanged avowals and now we had parted – forever. This would be the way always between us.

Rory was right. We could never meet without parting in anger.

Chapter Eleven

I HAD almost reached Gran's cottage when I heard swift footsteps following. Rory swept me into his arms. 'All right, you win. The choice is yours.' He added solemn words in Gaelic and, seeing my puzzled face, smiled. 'I forgot, you don't understand – and you part-Highland.'

'What did you say?'

He shrugged. 'For good or for evil, the die is cast.'

'Are you sure, Rory? Sure that you want to marry me? Do you really love me?'

He bent his head and kissed me and the cliff path, the sea-world beyond Clodha, spun like a top. 'Of course, I do.'

'Then it's all settled.'

But Rory shook his head. 'May, my darling, I still think you would be happier, in the long run, starting back for London by the next ferry to Oban. You would be safer too.'

'Safer?'

'That's what I said.' And he looked across the sea, brooding, searching the glistening waves.

'I don't understand, Rory.'

He shrugged. 'Marriage with me isn't going to be any bed of roses. It is a great pity you are not an islander. We should marry our own kind.'

'Marry your own kind, indeed. What nonsense. You talk as if the MacMhors are a different species of humans and Clodha a different world.' But even as I said the words I knew that secretly I thought so too. The fight at the quayside and some of Rory's ideas of democracy yesterday hardly belonged in the twentieth century.

'You will have to learn to take me – and Clodha – as you find us and keep rein on those reforming ideas,' he said sternly. 'We have been here a long time and we certainly cannot change for any woman's whim.' Then he laughed and took my hands, his face suddenly warm and eager. 'Let us see now. We can have the Ceilidh to celebrate our betrothal this Saturday and get married the following Sunday. That is the earliest we can get a minister from Oban. I will need to arrange for a special licence. It is a pity the minister only comes over to Clodha every Sunday fortnight or we could have been married earlier.'

'Married earlier,' I said. 'Do you really expect me to marry you in little more than a week from now?'

'Of course I do. Why the delay? Once it had been decided between us, and the betrothal announced, we should be married as soon as possible. Tomorrow would be perfect' – he drew me closer – 'or even tonight,' he whispered. 'Now what have I said? Why are you so shocked?'

'I'm not shocked. I love you. I want to be your wife as soon as possible too. But – these things take time to arrange.'

'Not on Clodha they don't. Or were you fancying a delicate three-year engagement with polite and conventional meetings in the respective family homes twice a year. I'm afraid, my darling, on

Clodha such behaviour would be regarded as quite abnormal. This is *our* way. Long courtships are barren, useless. Such refinements are merely for couples with leisure − and, I might add, with not much burning desire for each other. Engagements as you know them are only for the very young who have not yet a home of their own.'

Where was my dream of a white wedding, like all my other friends carefully planned to the last detail months ahead? The honeymoon hotel booked in some exotic setting, the reception that every bride dreams about, to proudly show off her new husband?

'Before this modern world caught up with us,' Rory was saying, 'there would have been no need for the church's blessing. All that was necessary was for us to declare ourselves man and wife three times before witnesses, there would have been none of this primitive giving and taking and offering up a woman in a white gown as a virgin sacrifice. Why should I wait? I have chosen you. I have a home up there' − he pointed to Castle Clodha − 'to offer. There is nothing I cannot give you until next year or the year after that, that I cannot offer you next Sunday. It is not as though you had London relatives to consult ...'

'I have a friend, Sarah. I told you about her. I'd love to have her at our wedding.'

'Very well. Invite her, by all means.'

'And what if she can't manage Sunday week? It is a long way, it is short notice ...'

'May, darling girl,' said Rory, 'is it me you want or your friend Sarah? What matter if she can't be here, she can visit us later ...'

'Rory, I promised she could be my bridesmaid.'

'But Katrine will be pleased to perform that duty for you,' said Rory cheerfully, and I thought, How horrible, he has no idea that she loves him. 'The actual wedding ceremony will be very quiet and short. The real celebration will be at the Ceilidh this Saturday, that will continue until the island runs dry. In the old days it took the place, I'm afraid, of the Church's blessing.'

It was noon when I went back to

184

Gran's cottage. This time yesterday I waited for the ferry in the rain at Oban, with nothing by my insubstantial dreams of Rory MacMhor. Today we were betrothed. In less than two weeks I would be his bride.

There was an odd silence over the dinner-table that day. Gran darted strange glances at me, as if she wanted to say something and couldn't find the right words. Katrine had failed to keep up the bantering tone with which she greeted my return and ate in glum silence.

When I came in she had been waiting for me. Hands on hips, she said: 'And now, aren't you the sly one, May Lachlan? I suppose congratulations are in order on being the fastest worker we have seen on Clodha for many a long day. Here's myself knowing Rory MacMhor for nearly thirty years and you got further with him in twenty-four hours than I did in all that time.' Her eyes raked over me contemptuously. 'How on earth did *you* do it?'

'Honestly, Katrine – I didn't mean to . . .'

'Of course you didn't,' she said sweetly. 'Rory did all the running, I'm sure, even persuading you to sleep with him at the hotel in Oban last night . . .'

'You're quite wrong, Katrine. I slept in the small bedroom of the MacMhor suite because there wasn't a bed to be had in Oban . . .'

Her dark eyebrows raised scornfully. 'Oh, really. Then it must have been a most interesting and fruitful day long before that.'

I didn't blame her. Who would? All her hopes of Rory had been dashed to the ground by a stranger, a cousin on holiday. All the years of struggling to make Rory love her, of doing things for him, of pretending that she really mattered, meant absolutely nothing on the day he fell in love with another girl.

What could anyone say but 'I'm sorry'?

She laughed harshly. 'Sorry for me? There is no need for you to be sorry for me. Actually you've done me a good turn. Helped me to make up my mind.'

'You mean you'll marry Colin, after all?'

'Possibly,' she said softly.

Yet I was sure it was Rory Katrine loved and I couldn't believe that she should change so quickly. I hoped for her sake and Colin's that this sudden decision wasn't the rebound of her disappointment over Rory.

'You realise, of course, May, why Rory asked you to marry him?'

'Well, I hope I do.'

She laughed. 'Don't imagine that he's in love with you. Rory's not the marrying type' – and I remembered he had used those very words – 'he's not capable of falling in love with anyone – believe me, because I know him better than you do. He's incapable of giving himself completely to anything – except Clodha. Clodha he worships, but he must provide sons if Colin doesn't beat him to it and it would break his heart to see his beloved island the property of his hated cousin and nephews still unborn. Even when he was engaged before it was only out of duty to Clodha. He never loved her, not really.' She paused. 'However, he does love – and need – money desperately, and I expect you told

187

him all about the legacy you expect from your father's friend.' She looked at me slowly. 'Don't completely set aside the possibility that he's marrying you because he thinks you're an heiress.'

'Katrine – don't be absurd,' I said indignantly. 'Good heavens, it may turn out to be only a few pounds.'

'Absurd, you say? It isn't absurd, I know what I'm talking about, and, believe me, I know Rory a lot better than you do, May,' she added in injured tones. 'Do you think it was really love that decided him to marry that plain little cousin from Perth?' She waited dramatically. 'Of course it wasn't. It was her money. And when it all ended so tragically, practically on the eve of their wedding, he managed to console himself very nicely on the money she left him. . . .'

Katrine turned and saw Gran. I wondered how much she had overheard, for she was standing at the door with the intent expression of one who listens without the slightest intention of missing a word.

'I want to talk to May,' she said

sternly, and I felt the new warmth we had achieved when she was ill had all drained away. This old woman regarded me with the harsh unfriendly eyes of a stranger.

'All right, Katrine, you can go,' she said sharply.

When the door had banged furiously shut I said: 'I'm sorry, Gran. I know what you must be thinking about my behaviour, but it isn't true . . .'

Gran held up her hand and laughed, her eyes suddenly young again. 'If you mean, do I believe all this daft chatter about you spending the night with Rory in Oban? Then the answer is – yes.' When I opened my mouth to protest she said: 'Don't interrupt. As you were in love with each other and intended marriage, then it was only right and proper – and what is more, completely natural. In Clodha morality *that* was your true marriage, all this getting a special licence and waiting for the minister to come over and bless you is a mere formality.'

Beaming, she shook an admonishing finger at me. 'So you thought I might be

189

angry? Och, away with you, I know Rory MacMhor too well . . .'

I heard the words with an ominous feeling that they were cropping up with monotonous regularity. Everyone, it seemed, on Clodha knew Rory too well except me.

'He's no seducer of young girls,' she continued. 'All the woman-chasing in this generation of MacMhors is done by Colin. And that could be speedily ended if Katrine had sense enough to recognise real love when it's under her very nose. He's always been daft about her, it's Katrine he really wants, the other girls – well, it's his way of bravado, of trying to make her jealous. Maybe she'll realise it now that Rory is out of her life. I hope so, anyway. Aye,' she added smiling, 'I'm not at all ill-pleased, child, by the way things have worked out. And it means that I may keep some of my own kin on Clodha too. You're a fine lass, May Lachlan, your blood is good and I'm proud of you.'

She took me in her arms and hugged me, then holding me at arm's length she said: 'Aye, you look healthy enough, for all your foreign breeding. Perhaps I'll have a great-grandson one day not too far off, who will be chief of MacMhor after I'm gone.'

When Katrine came downstairs again she seemed to have recovered from her anger and disappointment. She gave us a fashion parade of the new clothes her mother had bought her in Glasgow and her dark beauty was more dazzling than ever.

'How would it please you, Gran, if I said I was going to save some of these clothes for *my* trousseau?' she said.

Gran took her hands. 'Then I'd say, Katrine Lachlan, you were a wise lass to have come to your senses after all these years.'

Later, when Katrine fed the hens and I helped Gran wash-up, she gave a deep sigh of happiness. 'You know, child, I could be completely content to die this very moment, the way things have worked out. If only we did not have this curse of Clodha hanging over our heads, then I could be entirely happy.' She sighed and looked at me sadly. 'It seems Clodha was destined for you, even before you met Rory MacMhor. After all, Tanoth saw it all,' she reminded me.

In my new-found happiness I had almost forgotten that Tanoth had prophesied that I should 'die on Clodha'. How wonderful if I could dismiss it as dying here at the end of a long and useful life, an old woman and Rory's wife. But then with a chill at my heart I remembered the other words Tanoth had spoken:

Had Tanoth really supernatural powers? Was it possible that she or anyone else could have known that first night when we met that I was destined to be Rory MacMhor's bride?

'Doesn't it worry you at all?' asked Gran.

'Not in the slightest,' I lied cheerfully.

Not a thousand deaths, I said to myself, could spoil the sweetness of my love for Rory, or the wonder of being his chosen bride.

I rushed off a hasty letter to Sarah, begging her to come in time for my wedding and as I sealed it I remembered the last time I had seen her, when I closed the door of my old home for ever, and the horrifying feeling that overwhelmed me. That I would never return, that London, my home, Sarah and her boutique, were already part of the past.

Katrine's decision to marry Colin had obviously softened her heart towards me, for as I dressed to meet Rory she said: 'Now that you'll be going back and forth to Castle Clodha so frequently, I'll make you a present of that old bike of mine. It needs a bit of attention . . .'

'Katrine, that's too kind of you . . .'

'Rubbish,' she said. 'With the car now I never use it, I hate the wretched thing; besides, it's just going rusty. Come and I'll show you how to repair a puncture for a start.'

After patiently demonstrating the repair she wheeled the bike out and said: 'This front wheel has a bit of a wobble on it. It's really ready for scrap, but I dare say you won't be needing it much after – after the wedding.' And when I attempted to thank her again she said shortly: 'Shut up – you're doing me a favour . . .'

I didn't use it that evening, as Rory

came down in the car. He was tired and yawned a lot, explaining that he had been busy all day arranging the Ceilidh. 'We are to have it in the forecourt of the disused part of the castle and serve food from the kitchen. Then if it rains – well, we can adjourn to the long gallery . . .'

I listened to his plans with a growing sense of bewilderment. None of it had any feeling of reality – I couldn't believe that people would dance and sing and drink at Castle Clodha, celebrating on my behalf. Always when I closed my eyes I would see the forecourt of the castle, cold and grey and deserted, with the sky full of seagulls crying and a bitter wind blowing in from the Atlantic.

This evening, the first of our betrothal, was not a particularly successful one. Apart from the Ceilidh, neither of us had much conversation to contribute, as if during the past twenty-four hours we had talked ourselves out, and with sudden panic I wondered what we would talk about in the rest of our lives together. Then I realised that perhaps all newly engaged couples suffered this bout of sudden shyness.

Rory yawned again and I too pleaded tiredness and I felt his goodnight kiss was tinged with relief, especially when he added solemnly:

'I still think you ought to get on the next ferry out of Clodha.'

It was hardly the romantic ending I had envisaged for this particular evening, and I said, a little hurt and angry: 'You're certainly pressing the departure line rather heavily. There seems little point in getting married if you think I ought to sail away to Oban by the next ferry.' I sounded irritable and felt it. Where was all the magic that had been between us yesterday in Oban? Had it died forever or suffered only a temporary setback in a dose of premarital nerves?

Rory laughed and took me in his arms. A few kisses later, he sighed. 'You still don't realise what you're taking on, you're as sweet and innocent as that new-born lamb I found you rescuing — remember —' he added, as if I could ever forget, 'that first time we met? With every force set against you, but in true British stiff-upper-lip style, you'll sit it out.' But as I got out of the car, he said anxiously: 'Do take care, May. And I do love you.'

As I watched him drive away, it was all the reward I needed and I went to bed happy and carefree. After all, there would be other nights, we had the whole of our lives together.

Chapter Twelve

GRAN was still awake. She called to me as I tiptoed past her bedroom door. Too excited to sleep, thrilled and proud at the prospect of *her* grand-daughter becoming an island bride, particularly the bride of the chief of MacMhor, I was no longer a foreigner. I was reinstated as a Lachlan and she delivered a long lecture on island etiquette.

As Mrs. Rory MacMhor there were a bewildering number of occasions when I must always be present – if in health. For instance, I must be the first, after the immediate family, to hold each new-born baby on Clodha. Besides a vast number of birthdays and historical anniversaries to be remembered and contributed to, my help would be constantly sought for all manner of problems, financial and personal, among the womenfolk on the island.

'In fact,' said Gran, 'as Mrs. MacMhor you will become the foster-mother to more than a couple of hundred islanders. And you must be careful to find out what families are not speaking to each other, for they will watch you and if you talk longer to one family than their rivals it will be suspected that you are taking sides. Aye – but Rory will be telling you all this in due course.'

She patted my hand. 'I'm fine pleased that Rory has chosen you. There has never been a Lachlan and a MacMhor married for three generations now. It's good blood you have, child. Let us hope you will have fine sons and pray that you will see them to grown manhood,' she ended anxiously.

'Now, Gran, do stop worrying about a silly legend. I'm not worried – not in the least. After all, love is stronger than evil.'

She gave me an approving look. 'So

the Bible would have us believe. Well, well, perhaps they will be satisfied with poor Isobel and the curse of Clodha will not be looking in the direction of his second betrothed. But just you be careful, child. Oh, I almost forgot, there on the table, Tanoth left something for you.'

I picked up a tiny leather bag on a chain. 'Wear it. Tanoth said you are to wear it around your neck to keep off the evil eye.'

'How did she know about Rory and me so quickly?'

'Och, news fairly travels on Clodha,' said Gran, chuckling. 'And Tanoth has her own ways of finding out things. She told me she knew something like this was coming to Clodha when you first arrived.'

So her warning of danger *was* concerned with Rory and I turned suddenly cold inside. Hadn't she warned I would 'die on Clodha'? But would it be at the end of a long life shared with Rory or horribly, by a cruel and tragic accident, as Isobel had died? Listening to Gran, I shook myself free of my sad

198

thoughts. What did it matter, what cared I for time? Like all those in love, it was loving that mattered, one day or an eternity with Rory, both were measureless by man's concept of time.

Next morning, with the wind too fierce to contemplate pushing Katrine's bike up the hill, I hurried to the castle to help Rory prepare for the Ceilidh, wishing as I posted a letter to Sarah with my sensational news, that I could be there to see her face as she read it.

'When do we start?' I asked Rory, surprised to see me so early in the morning.

'When do we start on what? Have some coffee?'

'The preparations for the Ceilidh . . .'

'*We* don't do anything. The plans are settled, everything is smoothly under way.'

'But can't I help?' I asked, feeling disappointed at being deprived of the excitement of preparing my own engagement party.

'My dear lamb, the bride does nothing on such occasions, it is not to be expected of her. All she does is look pretty,' he drew me close and stroked back my hair, 'and it seems you won't have to try very hard to achieve that,' he added, kissing me gently. 'Och, there are plenty of women on Clodha who do this kind of thing regularly. They would be shocked and offended if you offered to help.'

Arranging the business side of getting married, plus an imminent by-election on the mainland, kept Rory busy. Then there was the farm, so, apart from 'sparing' me a couple of hours each evening, I was left to my own devices. Alas, my own devices were few and in my highly strung excited condition I would have been better of some outlet – like hard work. Sometimes I blinked hard, sure I would wake up, finding it impossible to believe that in just over one week I would be married. Being 'engaged', I discovered, was rather an anticlimax, and, like being in love, was turning out to be a vastly different experience from those recounted by my various friends through the years at Sarah's boutique.

Surely our meetings should have been

tingled with passion, by wild delight. But the exasperating thing was that having 'won' me, Rory seemed well content with our few meetings, while I longed to be with him every minute of the day.

Gran tended to be tedious too. With romance in the air, she turned garrulous and talked endlessly about other Lachlans and their wedding Ceilidhs and how mine would outshine any of those she remembered. For no Lachlan had ever married a chief of MacMhor until now.

Katrine troubled my conscience, but my worries were happily without cause. For a while I walked warily, anticipating scenes, angry words. However, she was polite and helpful and I had no reason for complaint – if, as I suspected, something of our early friendship had vanished, and that impossible to recall – after all, Katrine had reason for being hurt. When I was in her company she put on an excellent pretence, talking about Colin, how he loved her, how she must give a definite 'yes'. All seemed well, but instinct warned me that poor Katrine was putting on a good act for my benefit.

'Aye,' said Gran, coming in at the end of one of Katrine's conversations about Colin, 'and so you should have given him a definite "yes", as you call it, half a dozen years back, instead of climbing on to the shelf to wait for, er' – she darted a look across the table, remembering my presence in time – 'someone else known to all.'

'What utter nonsense,' said Katrine, her eyes flashing anger for the first time. 'I simply wasn't ready for marriage.'

'Ready for marriage, indeed,' snorted Gran. 'I was ready for marriage at sixteen – aye, and earlier than that. What else is there for a girl on Clodha?'

But the door had banged furiously behind Katrine and I said anxiously, 'Don't scold her, Gran,' embarrassed and ashamed at Gran's well-meant attempts to parade me before Katrine as a good example. From a useless foreigner, a London girl, I had been transformed almost overnight by Rory's love into a paragon. Now Gran never tired of telling Katrine how well I had looked after the hens, going out in that terrible storm to look at them and 'fighting off rats single-handed' in the early morning hours.

Katrine, preparing the hens' food, said sulkily, and not without cause: 'It isn't my fault if I'm terrified of rats.

'I'm terrified of mice too and they're only a quarter the size.'

Gran sniffed. 'There were another three pullets dead this morning.'

'I know, I know. But I put down poison just the way Sandy showed me. If they won't eat the beastly stuff I can't help it.'

'I hope you put it well away from the hens. And that you wash your hands carefully afterwards. We don't want to wake up dead and poisoned in our beds,' she added sternly.

Katrine looked across at me and winked. 'I'll be careful, Gran,' she said solemnly.

Since the day Rory had announced our engagement, Katrine avoided Castle Clodha. 'That's your job, May. You had better learn to look after the place if you're going to live there. Quite frankly, I can't see you coping with it — no woman who has spent her life in a

203

suburban street could possibly envisage the difficulties of living in a castle.' She laughed harshly. 'No doubt that mad witch Tanoth will show you some magic ways of dealing with cold and dust and big empty rooms.'

The weather had been too windy to cycle up to the castle, but the day before the Ceilidh dawned clear, calm and bright – the blue sky, the warm sun, brought promises of joy.

When I reached the castle, and pushed the bicycle through the cobbled courtyard, Tanoth was already in the kitchen, a child-like figure surrounded by a vast amount of baking. She must have been about her tasks since dawn. Bread, scones, shortbread, cakes piled up everywhere. For a moment I suspected magic – there was something weird, fey, about so much energy contained in such a tiny creature. I looked around, half-expecting to see other pale faces surrounding us, summoned up perhaps from the strange tapestry in her cottage and following her up the hill, to do her bidding. . . .

Tanoth seemed overjoyed to see me.

This was our first meeting since Rory and I became engaged, and, laughing, she clasped her hands almost gleefully when she noticed I was wearing her charm about my neck.

'No harm – will come – wear it,' she said solemnly when I thanked her.

Rory came into the kitchen at that moment and, engaged for several days now or no, my heart still somersaulted when he appeared. I supposed that when I had been married ten years or more I would take his entrances and his exits without undue emotion, but now each time he went away I was left with an indescribable sense of loss.

'Tanoth doesn't need you here. Come along, you're just in her way, isn't she?' He said something in Gaelic to Tanoth and put an arm around her shoulders and her gentle reply was accompanied by a look of sheer adoration. 'Come along, May, and I'll show you the setting for the Ceilidh.'

Hand in hand, we walked around to the ruined side of the castle, fronted by a great cobbled square. 'This is where the Clan MacMhor gathered for war in the old days. This is where our standard was raised for Charles in 1745, as it had been for his father, King James, in 1715. Men rode their horses up that flight of stairs and into the old chapel for blessing.'

The flight of steps now led to a crumbled lichen-covered wall. All that remained of the pre-Reformation church was a broken arch against the sky. Rory took my hand and led me through an old doorway into a smaller court, its flagstones overgrown with weeds. On our left were ruined stone stables and the remains of a tall grey tower.

'Have you a head for heights?' said Rory. 'Good. There's a marvellous view from the top of the tower.' As we walked across the flagstones, suddenly he seized my arm: 'Watch — May, that's the old well. You could have taken a nasty tumble there.'

I peered through a lichened grating and far below saw the glimmer of dark water. The smell of stagnation rose like a cloud on the wine-clear summer day.

As we walked across the floor of the stables, a faint beam of light shone down the worn stone tower-stairs. From the rafters above our heads a flock of birds rose screaming and vanished through the crumbled roof, furious at our intrusion, the floor under our feet springy as turf with nearly two hundred years of vitrified bird-droppings.

On the stairs our footsteps rang hollowly, up and up, to end in nothing but the lazy summer breeze and Castle Clodha far below. The cliff road lay like a grey ribbon and Clodha was a child's toy, a harbour with neat toy boats and white squares of houses glistening in sunlight, the sea a looking-glass, painted blue, and impossible to connect with anything as terrible as storms or waves or men drowning. Then, near the horizon, like a warning hand thrust out of a shining mirror, was Eilean na Gealach – the Isle of the Moon.

'Oh, Rory, how lovely it all is.'

Rory put his arm around me. 'Now it is all yours, May. This is your island, your people, your world too.' As he kissed me, he said: 'I have a present for you,' and from his pocket he took a heavy gold ring, ancient and crudely carved with the MacMhor coat of arms.

'This is the MacMhor betrothal ring. Too big? Ah, I was afraid of that. Don't worry, we'll have it altered when we go into Oban again,' he said, about to return it to his pocket.

'No, please, Rory. Don't take it back. Let me wear it. Look, it fits my index finger.'

Rory took my hand and kissed it and high on that windy place he held me close. The sigh he uttered was of pure happiness and I felt that every uncertainty between us had vanished never to return. At that moment I believed, as all lovers do, that love was eternal, that only death could part us, and I saw in a dream the years of our lives stretching before us, crowded with delights all yet to savour, and each one as happy as this moment together.

'I love you, May – so much. Don't run away back to London.'

I think if I could have died that moment I would have left the world content. 'Just you try sending me,' I said.

Rory held me tighter. 'Never again,' he whispered. 'I know when I'm beaten.'

And oblivious of our windy perch high

above Clodha, we kissed with passionate longing. Then we were negotiating the dark stair, blinded after the brightness we had left, and I was glad of Rory's guiding hand. In the little courtyard the sun blazed on empty stables, some with their stalls still visible, and I thought of the ghosts of horses, beloved horses, prancing, neighing with delight, their hoofs ringing on the cobblestones.

As though Rory read my mind, he said: 'Maybe I'll buy some horses again. Riding alone is a thing I have little taste for and the MacMhors have been notoriously unlucky in their dealings with horses. The wicked MacMhor, who starved Rowan to death in the turret room, had his neck broken when his horse threw him and the same unhappy fate befell my great-grandfather. However, our luck is going to change. We're going to change it, aren't we' — and he took my hands — 'May, my heart's darling?'

Leaving him later at the home farm, still wrapped in my cloud of love, I rode off on the bicycle, rather wobbly and insecure at first, but with growing confidence. It was a splendid feeling rushing downhill, carried on the wind, enjoying the scenery, dreaming of Rory . . .

Something was wrong. Terribly wrong. I had reached the steep corner near Tanoth's cottage where the cliff road fell away sharply. And I was going fast – much too fast. Wildly I pulled at the brakes.

Nothing happened. The cliff edge was coming – coming . . .

Vainly I tried to steer, to fling myself aside. There was a mighty crack and the whole wretched machine seemed to fall into pieces under me. Then I was hurtling into space – towards the cliff edge.

And even as I moved so swiftly, so horribly, to my doom, I saw it all like a terrible slow-moving film, the smooth grass, ruffled by the breeze, an old root of some forgotten bush, wizened grey . . .

My hand shot out. Some blind instinct of self-preservation – or was it Tanoth's charm? – the root was hurtling past, then with an agonising, sickening lurch that almost severed arm from socket and breath from body, I was clinging to it and my dangling feet touched rock. Dimly somewhere far above my head I heard a faint whirring sound and for a moment considered the wings of angels and guardian angels in particular. Then I realised what I heard was the whizzing of a bicycle wheel.

With a groan I opened one eye. Far below, the sea, blue and idle, breaking on a pebbled shore. I had landed by the miracle of the root on a narrow ledge, the cliff path mere inches above my head.

Before the misery of scratches, cuts and aches everywhere were clearly felt, my mind took in each detail of my surroundings. Great rocks far below. The waves like lace edging on a small stony beach where a man in shorts lay sunbathing, his arms flung wide to the sun. I gave a hysterical giggle at that. The man hadn't noticed me, perched wildly far above his head. He was sleeping there, probably snoring too, oblivious of my little drama. What a shock for him if I had zoomed down apparently from the sky, to land beside him.

Still laughing with mild hysteria, I clawed my way back to safety. Once on the road, my wounds began to smart sorely. The bicycle had disintegrated, my frantic cornering had wrenched off the front wheel.

Suddenly I felt such an idiot. Each time I had Katrine's bicycle I had an accident with it. Of course, I should have known better, for past history with even a junior cycle recalled two years of being eternally festooned with sticking plasters. At that moment I simply could not bear Katrine's 'you-are-a-fool' sigh, so I decided to sneak the poor wretched machine into Colin's garage and get a mechanic to repair it. I'd think of some excuse for its non-appearance.

Praying that I wouldn't meet anyone, I took the short cut down by the side of the fields, dragging the battered object by its one wheel, the other slung over my arm. By the time I reached the road to the garage, I was almost in tears, sore and aching all over. I was relieved when a car stopped and there was Colin.

'May — what on earth have you been

up to? And what is *that* contraption you've got with you. Oh, heavens – no, not Katrine's bike.' He was about to laugh, but, seeing my sorry condition, he opened the car door and said anxiously: 'In you get, can't send you home like that.'

Suddenly I began to cry and he took out a hanky and saying 'There, there,' he dried my tears. 'Poor little May, you have had a bad shaking. Never mind, never mind.' And he hugged me like a rather nice uncle. This was indeed another side of Colin MacMhor.

'I was hoping someone at the garage could fix up the bike before Katrine sees it.'

'Of course, of course. We'll try, but I can't promise. It looks like a write-off. Whatever happened?' When I told him he said: 'You certainly are lucky.'

'I'm sorry, but I don't feel lucky right now.'

He gave me a strange look. 'Consider it this way. You probably don't believe in such nonsense, but it looks rather as if the curse of Clodha is working overtime. After all, my cousin's first fiancée met her death on that very spot – she fell gathering wild flowers. It seems as if Rowan is growing rather impatient for her next victim ...'

Chapter Thirteen

COLIN lived in the house next to the garage, shared with his mother, on her rare visits home from the secretarial job which kept her in Glasgow – his mother, so despised by Gran for her 'city' ways. The house was attractively modern and could have fitted into the scene I had left in London, the first home on Clodha I had visited belonging even vaguely to the twentieth century.

Colin thrust a glass into my hand. 'Yes, you certainly were lucky to escape with a few cuts and bruises ...'

'What's this?' I asked.

'Whisky – what else? Go on, drink up – oh, for heaven's sake, *that*'s no way to sip it. Purely medicinal purposes' – he put a hand on his heart and said mockingly: 'I'm not trying to corrupt the morals of the bride-to-be — honestly. For once, you're quite safe with me.'

And watching him search for plasters and then gently bathing my cuts and scratches, the bowed head so like, yet so completely unlike, his cousin Rory, I felt the first tinge of pity for Colin MacMhor. There was nothing basically wrong with the man, but living in Rory's shadow all his life had somehow twisted him, like a tree growing away from the sun. At that moment I was certain that marriage with Katrine was a cure for all that ailed him.

'Sorry I won't be able to dance at your wedding,' he said, dabbing at a cut on my wrist. 'If there's one thing I hate to miss it's a good Ceilidh with the whisky flowing like water. That's really something to remember here on Clodha. However, I don't think Cousin Rory would be overjoyed at my presence — the skeleton at his feast, you might say.'

I felt distinctly uncomfortable, but knowing Rory's feelings towards his cousin, I could hardly be magnanimous and invite him.

215

'Heard from Felix Hall yet?' I asked, changing the subject.

Colin frowned. 'Not a word. Quite candidly, I'm worried. Something must have happened to him.'

There was a long pause. 'You're not seriously thinking Rory had something to do with it, are you?' I forced the words out, trying to give them a lightness, a mockery, I did not feel. I simply had to *know*.

He sat back on his heels and said soberly: 'I do indeed. And what is more,' he added, wagging a finger at me, 'so do you. Loyal little soul that you are, you think Rory had something to do with Felix's disappearance.'

'You're quite wrong, the thought never entered my mind,' I lied.

'Oh, come off it, you know by now, surely, that all the MacMhors are eminently capable of violence unlimited. Surely after witnessing that touching reunion of Rory and me down at the harbour you can't still have doubts that emotions live fairly close to the surface in the men of Clodha.'

'Anger perhaps, but not deliberate

murder. Not from Rory — I can't believe that.' I stood up. 'Thanks, Colin, for your first-aid treatment. I really must go.'

He laughed. 'That's always the woman's way out, isn't it? Just when something takes an interesting turn, she says: "I must go." ' As he opened the door, he said: 'Well, May, I'm sorry if it spoils your Ceilidh, but I'm notifying the police in Oban that Felix is missing if I don't hear from him by tomorrow.'

'What if he found something to amuse him on the mainland? He looked the kind of man who might be carried away very enthusiastically by a new project . . .'

Colin smiled. 'For project I think you also mean female.'

I shrugged. 'Perhaps someone else offered him an island to turn into a holiday camp, like Clodha, but without someone as stubborn as Rory to stand in his way.'

Colin shook his head. 'I would have known if there was something else in the air. Anyway, we aren't that cut off on Clodha. In reasonable weather there's the telephone and the post each day. I might be inclined to believe your theory – he might have got drunk and landed in some interesting situation – but there's only one thing disproves it.' He paused and added solemnly: 'Felix is one of the vainest, most fastidious, men I know – certainly not the kind of man to disappear for a mad weekend without taking a clean shirt.'

'What do you mean?'

Colin took my arm. 'I mean, you trusting innocent, that upstairs in the spare bedroom there is a large elegant suitcase, packed with clothes. Felix's travelling wardrobe – and I'm not altruistic enough to imagine he's bequeathed it to me as a present and rushed off shyly without saying he's not returning to claim it.

As we walked past the garage, I could think of no argument, remembering only and vividly the picture of Rory with rain-soaked hair and a rifle carefully wrapped in sacking under his arm. Rory with the face of a desperate man, the night of our broken date and Felix Hall's disappearance.

One of Colin's mechanics had the pieces of Katrine's bicycle spread out like a jigsaw. He looked up and said: 'The lassie will not be wanting this piece of iron just now, I'm hoping?' He shook his head sadly. 'Tch, tch, somebody really had their spite in for this poor auld machine.'

'I'll bring it over when it's mended,' said Colin with a laugh. 'Do your best with it, Dave.'

As we got into Colin's car, I said: 'I don't care if I never see it again. I never could ride anything on two wheels and I know now when I'm beaten. I've had quite enough – in future, I walk.'

Outside Gran's cottage, Colin switched off and turning to me said, 'Good luck, May. And I really mean that, whatever my personal feelings for cousin Rory. He's getting a lot better than he deserves, but that's just how I see it. I still wish you all the best. You're a fine lass and you'll not be having your troubles to seek, one way or another, taking on one of the wild MacMhors, I'm thinking.' He smiled. 'I expect I should bless you, anyway, for doing me a good turn. I suppose you realise by now that Rory and I were rivals for more than Clodha.'

'I know.'

Colin sighed. 'Och, well, perhaps Katrine will have me as a somewhat persistent second-best now.'

Later, peeling potatoes in the kitchen, I thought of Colin and his bad reputation. The one redeeming feature of his character the constant unchanging love he had showered on the heedless Katrine Lachlan all these years. Love which she had unashamedly exploited to the utmost. Using it to arouse Rory's jealousy, and because Rory hated Colin, perhaps with the hope it would drive him into a loveless marriage with her, if only to spite his cousin.

Gran and Katrine exchanged significant glances when they saw evidence of my accident in the shape of sticking plasters I could not conceal and a rather stiff knee.

'Now understand this,' I told them sternly, 'it has nothing to do with the curse of Clodha – I just happen to be accident-prone on anything with two wheels . . .'

But I could see they weren't convinced. And neither was I. I slept badly that night, the victim of nightmares where the Isle of Clodha turned to quicksand beneath my feet. The wretched accident and its implications of the super-natural had undermined my morale more than I cared to admit. In addition, Sarah's reaction to my telegram had been a letter of some length, suggesting that I had taken leave of my senses.

Remembering Colin's remarks about the curse of Clodha and the significance that my cycling mishap had been on the exact spot where Isobel had fallen to her death, I decided not to mention the incident to Rory. Remembering, too, Katrine and Gran's ominous expressions and the strange silence with which they greeted my protests of a 'purely natural occurrence', it was not my intention to give Rory the slightest excuse for putting me on the next ferry homeward to safety.

The day of our Ceilidh dawned fair and bright and the whole island was *en fête*. By evening almost every adult who had health and strength to reach the castle gathered to dance and carouse in the old courtyard, high under the stars. A full moon obligingly swam in the cloudless sky, adding to both sea and land the beautiful unreality of a vividly lit stage set.

Grateful for the design and dressmaking training which had helped make Sarah's boutique a success, and aided by Katrine and an old sewing-machine, I had spent most of the day making my dress for the Ceilidh from several yards of beautiful wild silk that Gran produced. I suspected, and perhaps Katrine too, that this had been laid aside for Katrine's trousseau. However, we both sewed with goodwill and by evening I had a full-skirted traditional dress with tight-fitting bodice and wide sleeves copied from a photograph in Rory's study of what his mother had worn for her betrothal Ceilidh.

Katrine drove Gran and me to the castle and Rory solemnly added a wide ribbon of blue MacMhor tartan across my shoulder before he led me out to meet the guests. Gran, as the bride's only relative, had a special place of honour and her new prestige on the island had brought back a sparkle to her eyes, a youthful gaiety that bore no likeness at all to the stern tired old woman who had greeted me so coolly on my arrival at Clodha. In two weeks Gran had shed twenty years. In the course of the evening I even observed her daringly sipping whisky.

Whisky — Rory's capacity for absorbing it seemed endless and this wild laughing man skirling and dancing was another face of the usually sombre Rory I loved. Always graceful, he went through the intricate steps of the sword dance repeatedly to tumultuous applause, even if at the end of it his bow to the admiring audience was a little unsteady and his steps back to the laden tables faintly uneven.

He grasped my hand. 'Happy, darling?' he whispered.

'Very happy.' And no longer shy or undemonstrative, he leaned across and kissed me to the delight of his slightly tipsy clansmen.

The old courtyard, with its fires, its

trestles of food, in the background the glowering shadow of the ruined wing of the castle lit by soft moonlight – all as romantic an engagement party as any girl could wish for. At that moment I held the world in my arms, with everything I had ever wished for, every dream had come surprisingly, impossibly, true.

If only – if only, the odd feeling of being cast off in time did not persist. By closing my eyes I could be back in time – two hundred years ago – more even, the men in their kilts, the girls white-dressed with clan sashes. Could this exist in the same world that had been mine until two short weeks ago – the world of space travel, of heart transplants, of new frontiers in scientific research?

I shivered. What if tomorrow morning I awoke and the dancers were gone and only the sheep moved over the grass-covered ruins of Castle Clodha. I walked a few steps and felt as light as air. Was I too a shade among shades?

'Cold, darling? Come and dance,' said Rory, and his arm warm and alive had nothing to do with ghosts, with times past and dead. Looking at him, the depression that had overcome me so quickly as rapidly vanished. In full ceremonial dress of black velvet jacket, silver-buttoned, with a white shirt frill at neck and cuffs, the dress MacMhor kilt, he made a magnificent figure, and the *skean dhu* tucked into his stocking top might never have been used for anything but ornament.

Fancy had led me to a wild idea that I might be coldly living in a ghost-haunted world, in love with a man who had been dead for two hundred years or more, but as he caught me in his arms and we whirled around to a strathspey, I had never seen him so alive – the black thick hair, his dark handsome face like a sculptor's dream, his strange eyes their colour ever-changing, all enhanced by the gaiety around us.

As the last strains of music died away we walked over to the MacMhor table on its raised dais where Gran was holding court with some of the older couples. Acknowledging their greetings, Rory said: 'Here's me with an empty glass, and that' – he pointed to the full one which I had barely touched all evening – 'that is your very first. Come along, drink up.'

Obediently, trying not to make too sour a face, I took a sip, and away on the top of the tower, Sandy Lachlan, the postman, who tonight was the MacMhor piper, began to play. Spellbound, I listened. I had never heard bagpipes other than on records, now I knew that nothing but the great out-of-doors could ever do them justice. They needed the infinite heavens above, preferably by moonlight, with the sea, dark and encompassing, lapping tiny beaches and the smell of wild heather blowing in the wind.

'You aren't drinking,' said Rory, eyeing me over his glass.

I looked at the whisky with distaste, wondering if I dare ask for something milder. Even bitter lemon, for tonight I needed no intoxicants – I was drunk with sheer joy of living and loving. Paradise could offer nothing greater than this, my hour, on Clodha.

'Darling,' said Rory gently, 'that's no way to treat good whisky, as if it's going to poison you. This is the way,' and taking the glass he stood up and drank to the dregs.

In the silence, with the piper gone, the clansmen applauded.

A moment later Rory fell to the ground.

As he lay unmoving, I felt my evening had been ruined, I felt the magic drain away and disgust and repugnance take its place. Why on earth had he drunk himself insensible at a time like this, especially when, judging by Oban, he seemed to have such a good head for drink?

The men nearest to us made good-natured attempts to stand him on his feet again, some of them almost as tipsy as he. Then Sandy Lachlan, the pipes discarded, pushed them aside and knelt down beside him.

'Himself is not drunk, you fools. He's ill. Quick now, let's get him inside.'

I looked down at Rory's white unmoving face, the eyes closed and heard Katrine's horrified whisper behind me: 'Oh God – not Rory, not Rory.'

And Gran's whisper: 'That's the very

first time I've ever heard of Rory MacMhor being drunk and incapable.'

A big man, he was carried ominously, like the dead Prince in *Hamlet*, from the moonlit scene by Sandy and three of the other men. Somehow they got him into the castle and up the twisting spiral stairs and put him to bed.

There would be no more carousing. Anxiously the groups dispersed, Katrine took Gran home and half an hour later she was with me in the Laird's study, pacing the floor, her face as white as the man's in the bed upstairs. Numbed, horrified, I found I could still think of Katrine's suffering. One picture of her kept returning as she danced past in Rory's arms, and I averted my eyes from them, from the naked delight on her face. Eyes blissfully closed, she leaned against him, as if she too toyed with dreams that night, as if she believed for a brief moment that this Ceilidh was hers, the betrothal Ceilidh and Rory MacMhor — both belonged to her.

At last the panelled door opened and Sandy came into the study. 'He's been awfu' sick, I've never seen a man so ill, but he's a wee thing better now and insisting that there is no doctor to be called for him.' He put a hand on my shoulder. 'He's asking for you. Try to talk some sense into him. I do not care for all this illness, without a doctor.'

'That's all right, Sandy. It's all taken care of.' Katrine had promised to telephone herself while I made coffee in the kitchen. 'When's he coming?' I asked her.

'I — I couldn't get through,' she said, her voice shaking. 'I'll try again.'

'For heaven's sake — keep on trying.' And I rushed upstairs.

Rory lay back against the pillows, his face deathly pale.

He turned his head and smiled wanly. 'Darling, I'm sorry — will you ever forgive me for such an exhibition? I know you'll never believe me, but that was the very first time I have ever been sick through drinking whisky.' He shuddered. 'After that I feel like signing the pledge. As for passing out cold, that's new too. The MacMhors have an inbuilt mechanism for the national drink.' He sighed. 'I must be getting old or else I got the dregs of the barrel.'

I took his hand. 'Katrine's getting the doctor – we'll soon find out.'

He sat up weakly. 'Och, May, tell her not to bother, I'm fine now, just fine. I must have been out of practice or,' he smiled, 'just too drunk with love before I started ...'

Leaning over I kissed him. 'I know what you mean. Oh, Rory, I love you so much.'

'As I love you, my heart's darling.'

A moment later he said: 'Go tell Katrine not to get the poor doctor out of his bed and across the water, I'd be ashamed to have him coming out at this time to attend to the drunken MacMhor.' He sat up, face paling. 'Will you go now quickly, darling,' he added hastily, 'I think I'm going to be sick again.'

Protesting, I sent Katrine home and all night I held vigil in the Laird's study, occasionally looking in to see how Rory was. His colour improved and soon he was asleep. Downstairs by the fire I dozed, but all the time, waking or sleeping, I struggled against an idea that persistently drifted to the surface of my mind, unwilling as I was to recognise it.

My drink had poisoned Rory without a shadow of doubt.

My drink that had stood untouched on the table all evening. Untouched? I wondered. And the panelled walls seemed to close in around me. For it had made Rory so ill, anaesthetised as he was by a vast quantity of whisky beforehand and a large amount of food, what would have been the outcome for someone drinking that glass on an empty stomach, for I had been too excited all day to eat more than a sandwich at lunchtime?

It took little reasoning and a chilly sense of horror to know that I might have been the one lying ill and perhaps by the time I had been taken to Oban and a stomach pump set to work it would have been too late. Much too late.

Suddenly I laughed, rather hysterically. The curse of Clodha indeed. It takes physical hands to tamper with drinks. And throwing the cloak Rory wore with the kilt around my shoulders I ran unafraid through to the old courtyard. But alas I was too late. As in my dream the tables and the dancers were gone, only the sheep bleated forlornly, grey shadows in a greyer world, and stacked in cartons were the whisky glasses, my evidence, all neatly washed and put away.

Chapter Fourteen

TANOTH arrived at Castle Clodha at six that morning. Shy and retiring, I had seen little of her at the Ceilidh apart from serving food and drink. For a moment I considered Tanoth – but what would she have to gain?

I wandered over to the window. Looking down on Clodha, the island seemed deserted. No doubt those quiet houses held some very sore heads this morning. Upstairs Rory was still asleep. I washed my face and felt better. Better again, if I did something which kept my mind occupied.

'Among other quaint customs, I wrote to Sarah, 'I think they also distill their own whisky on Clodha. My future husband is a little under the weather this morning and while I write this is sleeping it off – I imagine he'll awake with the genuine ancestor of all hangovers. In the kitchen Tanoth, the witch-girl I told you about, is already busy clearing away vast quantities of food . . .' I stopped, wishing I had been in time to save Rory's whisky glass. Now I'd never know.

'I'm so disappointed you can't manage to come for the wedding. I agree, you must have been completely bowled over, and it is very short notice . . .' I paused to consider more elaborate excuses for the hastiness; anything to alleviate Sarah's warnings that I was always impulsive and her advice to come home and think it over in the cold light of London.

'Thank you for telling Mr Scott I'm staying at Clodha. That was a tactful gesture – coming from me he might have considered it a rather broad hint about the legacy (or whatever it is).'

Tanoth knocked on the door and smiled at me as she went up to Rory's bedroom carrying some noxious-looking concoction of herbs. She stopped long enough to indicate by mime that this was a cure for a hangover. If I ever got used to drinking island whisky in the years to come, doubtless I would be grateful personally for her services.

Again the door opened from the long gallery and Katrine appeared. 'How is he?' she asked, her face still shocked-looking, her eyes glazed.

'Nothing to worry about. He's fine, and he's slept most of the night.' I yawned. 'Which is more than I can say.'

Katrine closed her eyes. 'Thank God,' she whispered. 'Thank God that he is all right.'

We met Tanoth on the winding stair, and she gave Katrine a look of pure hate, quite out of keeping with her usual gentleness. It made me shiver — as if I had seen the Evil Eye at work. Katrine was frightened too. She gave an involuntary cry and rushed up ahead of me to the bedroom, where she stood looking down at Rory, her face drawn and pale.

'Why do you let that madwoman anywhere near him?' she whispered with a shudder.

'She's quite different with Rory and with me too, Katrine. Honestly, I've never had anything but kindness from her.'

'Just wait until you do – you won't forget it,' said Katrine ominously.

I laughed shakily. 'What have you ever done to make her hate you like that?'

'Me? Nothing. Nothing at all,' said Katrine sharply. 'But at least you saw how she hates me, how she doesn't even bother to conceal it,' she added triumphantly. 'Now maybe you'll believe me for a change, believe that she can be an enemy, instead of pretending that she's just a sweet simple soul. She's evil, I tell you, evil and cruel.'

'Ssh,' I said, as Rory stirred, 'you'll wake him.'

Together we looked anxiously at his sleeping face. But today he was no longer like wax, the colour was back in his face and as I pushed a lock of black hair away from his eyes, they flickered open, focussed uncertainly. Then he smiled like a small boy and, turning on

235

his side, slept again.

'There now,' I said to Katrine, who gave a sigh of relief, 'he'll be all right. You can stop worrying about him.'

Back downstairs in the study, she said miserably, crouching by the fire, 'I have had the most terrible night. Nobody knows the agony I've suffered. I was sure he was going to die.'

'I thought so too, I must admit, and then I realised that this was probably the usual ending to a Ceilidh on Clodha.' There was no point in worrying her any further by adding my conviction that someone had tried to poison him. 'Surely you've seen men as drunk as Rory on Clodha quite frequently,' I ended lightly.

'That wasn't ...' Katrine began, and suddenly stopped.

'Wasn't what?'

'Oh,' she shrugged, 'I mean, it wasn't just normal drinking. I'm sure of that. He must have had an attack – a seizure of some kind. Of course, he has been working far too hard lately, and then all this excitement of the wedding,' she added, with a reproachful look.

For a moment I considered confiding

my suspicions, then Tanoth came in to fix the fire. Katrine retreated to the other side of the room and Tanoth bending towards the fire turned, looked at me, and shook her head in what could only amount to a warning gesture. Again, the same gesture as, touching her lips, she mouthed: 'No.'

'Are you coming home with me now?' said Katrine, eager to be gone. 'I have the car.'

'No – I'll stay and look after Rory.'

'I hardly think you're needed with *her* around,' she said as the door closed behind Tanoth.

'I want to stay.'

Katrine looked as if she might argue, then she said quietly: 'All right. But I hope he'll be fine, May. If anything happened to Rory . . .' and she left the statement unfinished.

I went downstairs with her and returning to the kitchen alone I said to Tanoth: 'What didn't you want me to tell Katrine?'

Tanoth frowned and I repeated the question. But she merely smiled and indicated that she didn't understand me.

She took refuge in a flood of Gaelic and I went upstairs wondering if I had imagined the whole thing.

Rory finally awoke at lunchtime with all the symptoms of a first-class hangover. He needed very little persuading to remain in bed and only pleaded weakly that the curtains be drawn against the light streaming through the window, and that Tanoth and I would walk very quietly please — oh yes, and try not to have Shep barking unnecessarily.

A strangely silent afternoon followed, while I endeavoured to sort out glasses and dishes in the kitchen, to be returned to their respective owners. Tanoth working with me was more withdrawn than ever. Apart from an occasional smile she resisted all attempts at even our limited conversation. As time passed, when our glance met over some shared task I shivered. Her eyes had turned completely vacant and I had the oddest feeling of looking into an empty room whence the occupant had fled.

I made tea and took it up on a tray to Rory, but found I could not wake him. I felt rather irritated by this, although he looked so much better, for it seemed somehow inconsiderate to spend an entire day away from me just to sleep off a hangover. However, back in the kitchen I got the answer from Tanoth, who indicated by laying her face against her hands and an elaborate pantomime of stirring that the herbs she had given him were to make him sleep and had restorative powers. She also indicated in very clear fashion what I already suspected, that someone had tampered with his drink. The only thing she didn't know was that it was *mine*.

Tanoth went home and the castle seemed larger, gloomier. The long gallery echoed dolefully and the sun disappeared. Suddenly I began to feel ill-at-ease, as though faces watched me in the gloom. I shivered and put the uncomfortable feeling down to still wearing the white dress from the Ceilidh — if only Katrine had remembered, or I had asked her to bring a warm sweater and cardigan. I decided that perhaps a breath of fresh air was what I needed and throwing Rory's cloak around my shoulders I walked down the hill back to Gran's cottage.

Even though the day was cloudy, the air was sweet still. Strange, if it had not been for Rory and I falling in love this would have been the end of my holiday. Quite suddenly I thought how lucky, how immeasurably lucky, I had been and was at this moment, as I considered the other May, hopelessly loving Rory who would have been preparing to leave Clodha, full of misery and the terrible feeling that the end of the world had come, that she would never love anyone as much again. Such are the agonies of first love. Now that I had experienced them I felt at one with all those other famous lovers through history who had despaired and suffered and even died for love. I could have shaken hands at that moment with Lancelot and Guinevere, with Romeo and Juliet, and called them all soul-mates. Odd, I thought, that there must be far more happy lovers than sad ones, but only the tragic are remembered, those others who married, had children, and lived out long serene lives together, nobody thought worthy of recording.

Now I had Rory and Clodha. A month ago I had Sarah's boutique – and nothing. A great big empty 'O' of a world. Yet I had loved the boutique, the glamorous with-it clothes. Now all I wanted of that life was to see Sarah again. I pictured her coming to Clodha, staying with us at the castle and being completely captivated by Rory. Loving him as I did, it seemed impossible that any woman could resist him.

I stopped and thought of Katrine. Poor Katrine, she was the only one who had suffered through my romance with Rory. How would I have faced such a situation had I been in her place? Would I have managed to put such a calm face on it, or would I have been a screaming shrew, my nails outstretched ready to claw? I felt that Katrine had emerged from her love for Rory, that love of a lifetime, with dignity and honour. Perhaps, as she said, it made her see things more clearly. After all, had she really fared so badly? Rory had obviously never loved her and Colin had and did. Perhaps she was at this moment seeing herself far better off with Colin, that they were fundamentally more suited to each other.

But at that moment – where was Katrine? The door was locked and neither she nor Gran were anywhere in evidence. I presumed that Gran must be highly in demand now, the honoured visitor, and imagined her taking cups of tea in some remote cottage and mulling over the events of the Ceilidh. Really – it was very trying. Here I was in a silly white dress and a man's cloak and all my sensible clothes in a bedroom upstairs, its window closed and quite inaccessible from the ground.

Suddenly I began to laugh. It was all so idiotic. When I had so many things to be happy about what difference did it make what I wore – it was only for a few hours more. I felt happy and elated again at turning my steps towards Castle Clodha. I thought of Rory lying sleeping, waiting for me ... And everything was immediately rosy, the whole world my oyster. Why was I worrying unnecessarily – about *whose* drink Rory took before he collapsed? After all, nobody could prove that it had been tampered with, but anybody with eyes could see that Rory had imbibed very heavily before that last glass? Perhaps I was inventing morbid solutions to something that had been a mere idle remark, a mere piece of face-saving. After all, Rory MacMhor was a person of some importance. He had his prestige to protect, and a drunken man, even a drunken chief of a proud clan, loses just a fragment of his dignity.

The curse of Clodha indeed. A silly superstition. This was the twentieth century, the space age, where everything had to have a scientific explanation....

I had been walking rapidly. Now I slowed down. Surely this was the exact spot on the cliff road where I had the accident with Katrine's bicycle. Yes — over there the skid marks gouged into the verge. And there, a few yards further, something gleamed in the grass. A fragment of the bell which I hadn't noticed as I gathered the wrecked machine together.

As I picked it up, I was on the edge of the cliff again and out of sheer morbid delight at my lucky escape I looked down. . . .

It was all as it had been yesterday, the broken root I had seized, and there, far below the sharp rocks, the tiny pebbled beach with the waves lapping.

The scene was complete, right down to the man sunbathing. He was in exactly the same position as I had first observed him, only the back of his head visible, his face turned towards the sea.

Sunbathing – that was surely odd. I looked at the sky. There was no sun today, in fact the air was distinctly chilly, but there was the sunbather on the pebbled beach, his arms outflung.

And suddenly my feet prickled with danger, with horror. It was no man sunbathing I looked down on . . . *That was a drowned man.*

Fighting back nausea, I leaned over the cliff edge and tried to see him more clearly. Of course, now it was all quite clear, he had been washed into the cove and hidden by the rocks from the sight of anyone passing in a boat. Lying just below the cliff-face itself, he wouldn't be apparent to anyone walking or driving up and down the road unless they came, as I did, and leaned *right* over on hands and knees.

I looked again. He was wearing trunks of some kind and dark goggles. A big white body, rather flabby, but I couldn't make out the face from this distance.

A big man, paunchy, middle-aged. And sickness rose into my throat as I thought of Felix Hall, picturing Rory killing him, stripping the body and pushing it into the sea to make it look like a drowning accident. . . .

I jumped to my feet and began to run down the road back to the harbour. Colin was there tinkering with his speedboat. I must tell him. He would know what to do.

He looked up and smiled and the words stuck in my throat.

I said: 'I'm locked out of the cottage. Gran and Katrine must be away somewhere.'

He grinned. 'I wondered what the fancy dress was for? Sorry I can't help. I saw Katrine driving with Gran to the other side of the island hours ago. They had boxes with them, probably returning some of the borrowed crockery from last night, or playing Ladies Bountiful with the leftovers. They should be back soon.' He straightened up. 'I'm glad to see you've recovered. Hear you almost had a tragedy — someone tried to poison cousin Rory at last.' He laughed bitterly. 'Good job I wasn't anywhere in the vicinity — and I can prove it. I might have been the prime suspect — in fact, had this situation happened in less civilised days, for touching with evil intent the chief of MacMhor's sacred person, I'd probably be hanging from the nearest tree by now.'

'Where did you get the idea that someone tried to poison Rory?' I asked, the coldness inside me growing, the importance of the drowned man in the cove receding.

Colin shrugged. 'Just a figure of speech. Heavens, girl, I'm only teasing. You are touchy today.'

'I'm sorry.'

'Are you just a little bit hung-over too?'

'Not on my incapacity for alcohol — I don't go looking for trouble.'

'Nor does Rory. It sounds completely out of character that Rory should collapse at his own Ceilidh when he can outdrink any man on the island, including me,' he added reluctantly. 'Perhaps we're in for a change of scene and it's the male of the MacMhor species instead of their unfortunate wives who is to be cursed for a change.'

'Don't be hateful. When you say things like that I begin to wonder if Rory was poisoned, couldn't it possibly have been you?' I said sweetly. 'After all, you could have arranged it − and you do have most to gain if anything happens to him.'

'For heaven's sake, May. I'm only teasing.' Then he added sulkily, 'With Felix missing, I wouldn't be one whit better off now as the chief of MacMhor.'

'So Felix Hall is still missing. Any ideas where he might be?' I tried to make the words sound light, but they came out heavy as doom.

'Not the faintest. I notified the police in Oban this morning that he was a missing person.' He looked at me slowly. 'I hope your wedding festivities won't be interrupted by a great bevy of bobbies coming to cart the bridegroom away. As is done, you'll no doubt remember, in all the best ballads.'

'Why should they want Rory?' The words were leaden.

'Oh, don't be so naive. You know perfectly well that Rory would be delighted to have Felix Hall at the bottom of the sea right now.'

Or the bottom of the cliff, I thought grimly. I was glad I hadn't rushed to tell Colin — perhaps I had gained Rory a day, or even the few hours, that would be all necessary for him to put safety between himself and Clodha. If only I could warn him in time . . .

'Where are you off to in such a hurry?' asked Colin. 'Stay and talk to me for a while. I'm just away below to brew some coffee — oh come on, stay and have a cup.'

'No, really — I must go. Rory might need me.'

'Oh, I see. The fond lovers — ah well. Here, May, you take it easy. You're looking rather poorly — sick nursing doesn't seem to agree with you . . .'

I left him mid-sentence, thinking of Rory lying asleep up there in the castle, quite oblivious of discovery. Of the net closing. Of the dead man lying just a few hundred yards away from us.

As Colin talked, I knew I had made my decision. Right or wrong, Rory must be warned. He must have his chance. I thanked heaven that Colin had told me Felix was officially missing before I told him what I had seen.

I walked quickly back to the cottage, but its occupants hadn't returned. As I closed the gate, Colin's mechanic with a car on tow leaned out of the repair van's window:

'Wanting your bike back, are you?'

'I'm in no hurry for it.'

'Aye, and a good job, too. Someone must have gone for that front wheel with a crowbar. Lassies should leave repairs to the experts,' he added reproachfully. 'And the brakes were practically cut through as well ... Aye, but that was a fine Ceilidh, and how's Himself today?'

I answered briefly but politely, longing to be on my way. I had too many other things on my mind for a pleasant gossip

249

and so it wasn't until very much later that the significance of his remarks fitted into the pattern.

Chapter Fifteen

BY the time I reached Castle Clodha, I had rehearsed and discarded a dozen speeches, warning Rory that Felix Hall's body had been discovered. Presumably drowning would be assumed until the post-mortem revealed evidence of foul play. Strange how primitive emotions can change us. I had been reared to painful honesty where even cheating the corporation transport of a sixpenny fare would have appalled me. Yet here I was running through the long galley, capable of shielding a murderer and already preparing an alibi, contemplating perjury, without a single qualm, because the man I loved was in danger.

The Laird's study, the bedroom — both were empty. Calling Rory, I ran downstairs into the kitchen, frantic now because I could not find him. He had gone out, but where? – and it had never occurred to him to leave a note. He would naturally think that I had returned to Gran's while he slept.

I tried to think where to begin my urgent search. Perhaps at the home farm? Calmness was essential, but like a rat trapped in a cage I wanted to rush off in several different directions at once.

At that moment the telephone rang and trembling I lifted the receiver. 'Is that you, May? Katrine here. Come at once, will you – to the Tower. Rory's been hurt.'

'Hurt? How? What happened . . .?'

'Don't waste time asking questions. Just *come*.'

'Katrine? Wait – Katrine.' But the line went dead. I had a prickling awful sense of inevitable disaster. Katrine sounded so odd, her voice far away, muffled, hoarse – almost unrecognisable.

Throwing Rory's cloak around my shoulders again, and hating that ridiculous white dress, now so crushed and limp and also chilly, I rushed through the little courtyard and around to the disused part of the castle, the scene of last night's Ceilidh.

Only the bruised grass bore witness to our revelry. Dusk was rapidly encroaching and everything was strangely silent, the world of Clodha sleeping. Heavy clouds raced across the moon's face as if another storm was on the way and far below, the sea was ribboned by white foam. There was another feeling in the air tonight, something I had brought with me, to do with my own fears that Rory had murdered Felix Hall. The smell, the tangible feeling of danger.

The whole scene before me apart from my instinct for disaster was unreal. My sandalled feet made no noise on the cobblestones and I felt like a ghost among ghosts. The stables stood darkly, a grey outline against the paler grey of gloaming. They were undoubtedly haunted, the tower above them grim and uninviting.

Beneath my feet a sea of waving fronds of weeds had obliterated the flagstones. This, I thought, is what it must be like to come back as a spirit to haunt old places — no wonder ghosts are always unhappy and restless.

'Katrine, Rory,' I called. 'Where are you?'

There was no reply. 'Rory — it's me, May.'

Why didn't they answer? And even as I ran across the uneven stones I thought how strange Katrine's voice had been, so unlike her clear bell-like tones. I regarded the tower with distaste and fear. Was Katrine waiting for me at the top of those frail stones with nothing but the wind around her and the ground sickeningly far below? How safe I had felt in Rory's arms, and suddenly I was afraid, not wanting to go up in the dark and find Katrine waiting for me there.

What if the phone call had been a hoax? What if someone wanted me out here for their own sinister purpose?

I wondered if I had said the words out loud, for they seemed to echo in the air. Danger. Danger.

And almost as if someone had seized my arm, I jerked to a standstill, every nerve tingling, every instinct quivering with the sense of disaster.

'Katrine – Rory,' I called again.

Now I stepped forward cautiously and looked down at my feet. Where the flagstones ceased just beyond my toes, and almost hidden by weeds, a great chasm yawned. With a cold tingle of fear, I remembered Rory's words: 'Watch out for the well.'

But last time I had only been in danger of a ricked ankle. Last time there had been a grating. Tonight there was none, nothing but the round hole and far below the glimmer and stench of stagnant water. One step more and I would have hurtled down, down – screaming – to die horribly in the slimy green depths.

'Katrine,' I whispered into the darkness. 'Rory. Rory.'

What if one, or both, had fallen down and were already as dead as the man on the beach? Or what if Rory lay injured on the tower and Katrine running for help had fallen down the well?

And then the whole fallibility of the scheme reached out and took me by the throat. If I hadn't been in such a panic about warning Rory and predisposed for

Katrine's call, surely I would have realised that the nearest telephone for someone in the direction of the tower here was the phone in Castle Clodha? After that the nearest call-box was at the home farm. But why should Katrine bother to go there when she could have run through the courtyard and into the castle and met me face to face?

The answer was obviously that the caller was not Katrine. Who then? I had to find out. Rory might be in danger, perhaps even dying. Perhaps the poisoner of last night, displeased with the unsatisfactory results, had lured Rory out of Castle Clodha on some pretence of urgency – one reason why he had disappeared without leaving a note. Had he too been invited to an assignation on the tower and had the caller used me as bait?

Above my head the tower loomed ugly, frightening, a thing from nightmare. With shaking legs I ran up the steps, feeling my way. At last there was only the sky above with the wind and the lights gleaming like a necklace on the mainland far across the dark sea, the world of Clodha and myself deserted by all other living kind.

I came back down feeling as if the fingers of doom were scratching at the back of my neck, wondering in a kind of growing horror where I would search next. But when I reached the study there was Rory, frowning over a letter at his desk.

Rory. My own danger at the well was eclipsed completely by his imminent danger of discovery. I looked at him and my heart constricted. Rory whom I loved with all my heart – Rory who had killed a man in cold blood. Where, oh where, did I find the words to tell him that I knew?

Incredible that he should be oblivious of it all, smiling at me, smiling as if the world – our world – would go on sweetly and kindly in Clodha's sunrise and sunset and not turn to ashes at our feet.

Rory, you killed Felix Hall. There were the words but where was the courage needed to utter them? Like a mother whose child by its own folly has narrowly escaped a fatal accident, I took refuge in anger:

'Where have you been? I looked everywhere for you.'

He looked surprised as well he might, for the role of nagging woman was new to me. 'I had a walk. Beyond the spinney,' he said apologetically. 'All that was needed was some fresh air to clear my head. Yes, of course, I've recovered. Feel great.' Picking up some papers, he nodded towards the telephone. 'You just missed Katrine. She called to ask after the poor invalid. What a fuss about a hangover.'

I leaned against the table, weak with relief that Katrine wasn't at the bottom of the well and Rory was fit − and alive. Now all that remained was to say: I know you killed Felix Hall, but I love you and I'll help you to escape the law.

The words were too awful. Wasn't there anything to soften them? What about all the books I had read with similar situations, the films I had seen? I thought frantically but no cushioned words came.

Taking a deep breath, I began. 'Rory ...'

He came over smiling and kissed me.

257

'There, there, darling. No need to get in a panic. I'm all right, quite fit again. Nothing to look mournful about, is there?'

Now was my chance. I know you killed Felix Hall. Instead I heard myself gabbling nervously: 'I went to the cottage to change into my other clothes and Gran wasn't in. The door was locked.'

'But you look beautiful like that,' said Rory, narrowing his eyes. 'That is how I shall always remember you. In the white dress with the MacMhor tartan sash. You were so lovely.'

The words 'always remember' had a sombre ring. I wondered why he was already talking about us — about our love — as if it belonged in the past. You have so little time, time, time, ticked the clock on the shelf, reminding me of the warning for Rory. Perhaps I was already too late and the brief golden dream we had shared together had vanished to the four winds. I saw myself plainly going back to Oban, then to London. I saw my life shattered beyond hope of resurrection.

Rory had certainly made a spectacular recovery. He put an arm around me and didn't notice that I failed to return his kiss. He was preoccupied, looking at the desk. Frowning, he picked up a pen and said: 'Sit down for a moment, May. I have some bills to pay – just a few cheques to write.'

'Rory,' I began desperately.

'Let me take that cloak, heavens – it weighs a ton. I'll get you a sweater if you're cold.' Removing the cloak from my shoulders, he said 'Hello' and lifted my left arm. 'What on earth is this?' I looked down at an enormous bruise.

'It must have happened last night – during the dancing, I expect.'

But Rory shook his head. 'This bruise is quite new.'

'Then I must have hit it going up the tower.' Touching it, I winced. It was extremely tender.

'The tower? What were you doing there?'

'When I came back from the cottage I couldn't find you anywhere and, just as I was leaving, Katrine phoned and said you had been hurt, you were in the tower. When I rushed up there to find you someone had taken the cover off the old well. I was almost killed – I don't know what stopped me . . .'

'A hand, perhaps,' said Rory, examining my arm. 'That isn't a bump, May – look, it's the mark of a hand, see – fingers and all. Someone must have taken you in one almighty grip.'

I walked over to the mirror and there quite plainly were four marks, like those of fingers on my upper arm. Someone – or something – had said the words I thought I heard.

'Someone – or something – saved me, Rory,' I whispered. And as I told him how *forcibly* I had jerked to a standstill, *as if my arm had been seized*, I lingered over it, taking cowardly refuge in yet another chance to delay my accusation, praying for a miracle. Otherwise, if a miracle did not exist, what had my life been saved for? To see Rory go to prison on a life sentence for murder?

'It seems incredible,' he said. 'Katrine phoned to ask how I was. She had been away with your grandmother to the other side of the island, distributing the remains of the feast to some of the poorer crofting families. Oh, May, it must have been a joke.'

'A joke,' I said furiously. 'Someone tried to kill me and you call that a joke.'

'Someone also saved your life, apparently. And what would you call that? Darling,' he added, with weary tolerance, 'don't you think you're exaggerating all this a wee bit? Couldn't you have imagined all that business at the tower? I think you've got our MacMhor legend rather on your mind, haven't you? Aren't you just a wee thing over-wrought? Engagement nerves and all that sort of thing.' He pulled on his jacket. 'Come along, let's see what caused all the trouble.'

He walked so quickly I needed all my breath to keep up with him. The whole situation was becoming more and more nightmarish. Maybe I was dreaming, maybe the cold air on my face was part of that dream. Any moment now the alarm would go off and I'd be back in the terraced house in London. There would be no Rory, whom I loved, and who was lost forever. . . .

We reached the courtyard and there in the flagstones beside the tower, as I knew it would be, the cover had been replaced on the well. And Rory was regarding me in evident disbelief, not angry, merely amused.

I blinked, hoping to wake up, but there was no escape from reality, from Rory's question: 'What was the real reason you came, May?'

'Because I thought you might be hurt – or in danger. I had to warn you.'

'Warn me? About what?' His voice was gentle, but he was suddenly very still, I suspected alert and watchful too, like animals who 'freeze' in the presence of danger. At that moment he was a complete stranger, sinister, Rory MacMhor no longer, but a dark shadow capable of anything, of murdering a man – or a woman – who stood in his way. If he had taken a dirk and stuck it in my throat I would not have been greatly surprised as I died.

'You're cold,' he said smoothly, 'and so am I. Let's discuss that warning over a cup of coffee.' He was laughing now, sure of himself again, pretending not to take it seriously. He took my arm and I pulled away from him sharply. Suddenly I didn't want to go into the castle with him alone. I wanted to run, away down the hill — run screaming, back to people I knew and understood, people who didn't feud and fight and have their lives haunted by curses and superstitions and witches.

In the kitchen he switched on the electric kettle. 'Well, what's all the fuss about? Has Westminster got their tax man on my heels again?' He had recovered his composure, the dark eyes were mocking but tolerant. They said plainly that I was an idiot, a silly hysterical girl who would never learn to cope with life on Clodha in a thousand years. You had to be tough and ruthless to survive here against the elements, against men's passions — and I was neither.

I watched this stranger I had loved measure coffee into two mugs. It was all so domesticated, almost cosy, and my words had no place in such a scene, or with the soft, gentle, loving things of life.

'You killed Felix Hall, didn't you?'

His hand never wavered. He made no sudden gesture. It was as if the words were no shock to him. Almost casually he switched off the boiling kettle, poured water on to the coffee, measured two spoonsful of sugar into his own mug. He sat on the edge of the table, took a few sips, and then in a long and terrible silence he turned slowly, looked at me. In that look pity intermingled with scorn, then just as rapidly his face cleared to an expression I knew, of gentle mockery.

'Isn't that a strange question to be asking me now?' he said softly. 'And would you, suspecting such a terrible thing, be willing still to marry me? Knowing all the time that you might be living with a murderer?'

'Colin suspects it. He thinks you had something to do with Hall's disappearance. The man left a whole case of clothes with Colin ...'

'Ah, Colin, is it? Colin suspects ...'

'Yes, he does. And he's informed the Oban police that Hall has disappeared. I shouldn't think Colin is the only one either. Think of all the other people on Clodha who saw you out looking for him with a gun the night he disappeared.'

'Most of them saw that I didn't find him either, unfortunately.'

'How can you say unfortunately – have you no respect for human life? Just because a man is in your way you can't brush him aside like a fly or a beetle ...'

Rory turned to face me slowly. 'May,' he said, his voice heavy with sudden weariness, 'I have many vices, but hypocrisy is not one of them. Nor is hospitality to people I feel have a corrupting influence on Clodha – on my land and my people.'

I couldn't find words to argue and the cold silence was worse than anything that had happened before. I felt the full horror of my clumsy questions and at that moment would have done anything, anything, to undo the terrible destructive power I had unleashed into our relationship.

'I only wanted to know for sure,' I said, searching for the right words, words that would never again be found between us.

Rory laughed bitterly. 'You seem to have a remarkable talent for believing everyone except me,' he said coldly. 'What difference would it make if I said yes or no, anyway?'

'If you said no, I would believe you.'

The dark eyebrows raised disdainfully. 'How very kind of you. A charming thought with which to begin our life together.'

'Rory,' I said desperately, 'I would still marry you even if you had killed Hall. Perhaps you were provoked, I don't know, perhaps it was an accident.' I seized his arms, but he stood unmoving, unyielding, and I might as well have seized a block of granite. 'Rory, Rory darling, I love you. That's all I know. And whatever you have done I'll lie and cheat to save you, I'll give you an alibi, we can go away from this, start some other life where no one knows you. Rory, I'll come with you to the ends of the earth — whatever you've done, if only you love me.'

He shook himself free from my grasp and poured water into the empty coffee mugs in the sink. He looked up and out of the window, down into the darkness that hid the rest of Clodha. 'I believe you would too, you loyal and devoted little soul. Unfortunately that isn't enough for me,' and his words fell like drops of ice on my heart. 'I really think, despite your very touching devotion, that you had better be on the next ferry to Oban in the morning. And when you are safely back in London you will have time then to count your blessings, especially the lucky escape you had from a lifetime with one of the wild MacMhors.'

He turned round and we stood looking into each other's eyes and there was nothing, nothing more to be said. In that moment love had plainly died. I knew tomorrow I would feel the pain, but tonight I was only tired, tired to the depths of my soul. All I wanted was oblivion, a few hours' respite before the numbness wore off and the agony of losing him began.

Shattering the silence between us, the telephone rang. Rory picked it up. 'Yes, of course. Where? Yes, yes. I'll come. Right away.' And replacing the receiver, he said, almost tenderly:

'If you were coming to warn me, May Lachlan, I'm afraid you left it too late.

Much too late. That was the Coastguard – they have found the body of a man at the bottom of the cliffs, just beyond the Castle here. Colin is on his way to identify the body now – he thinks it is Felix Hall.'

Chapter Sixteen

'IF you were coming to warn me . . . you left it too late . . . They have found the body of a man . . . Colin thinks it is Felix Hall . . .'

Almost twelve hours had passed since Rory and I parted, but the words lingered, words grown in enormity during the terrible night I had spent back in Gran's cottage, alone with my conscience.

The car must have already been on its way up to Castle Clodha when the telephone call was made to Rory. He had hardly replaced the receiver when the doorbell in the kitchen rang and following him downstairs, numbed into speechlessness, I found two policemen waiting. The interview was all very civilised and polite, carried on in hushed and reverent tones. They were merely informing him of the discovery on his land, etc., etc. ... Perhaps he would like to accompany them to Oban?

'All right, all right,' he said, as though impatient to get it over with. 'Can we give Miss Lachlan here a lift down the road?'

As I sat beside him in the back of the car, I stretched out and clasped his hand. It was cold and he made no sign that he was aware of my feeble gesture of comfort and reassurance as he stared unmoving out of the window. When the car stopped at Gran's cottage he turned his head briefly: 'Good night, May. Take some advice. Go home where you belong on the next ferry out of Clodha.'

The door closed and the car zoomed down the hill. I watched them go. Suddenly there was so much to say and all of it too late. As I walked past Gran's bedroom door she was snoring gently and I looked out of the window and saw light and busy activity at the harbour.

Boats and lights and a small crowd gathered. Presumably Katrine was there, but I had little desire to join the crowd of eager spectators. Wearily I went to bed and pretended to be asleep when hours later Katrine crept into the bedroom.

'Take some advice ... go home ... go home.' I lay remembering Rory's cold voice, the tired expressionless face that indicated more clearly than words that all was indeed over between us. Love had been murdered, too, that night.

It would be gross exaggeration to say that I awoke next morning, since most of the night I had lain with closed eyes reliving the sweetness of moments with Rory that had gone for ever. At last I heard five o'clock strike downstairs and by then I knew the decision had been reached. I knew exactly what I must do to make amends.

I loved him and would probably love him for ever, but I had destroyed all hope of happiness between us when I had practically accused him of murder. even now I was not one whit nearer knowing whether he was guilty or not. Loving him, my heart said he was incapable of such an action and silently accused me of the unforgivable wrong I had done him. And yet, and yet, whispered conscience, in retaliation, he had not denied it.

Perhaps I would never know the truth, but all that mattered was to leave Clodha before he returned from Oban. Without disturbing the still-sleeping Katrine, I left the cottage and climbed the hill to the castle for the last time. I scrawled a note: 'Have taken your advice. Goodbye.' This I would leave with the betrothal ring for him to find when he returned.

When I reached the castle, much to my surprise the kitchen door was unlocked. Rory must have overlooked it in his agitation last night. The kitchen was chilly and desolate, the mugs we had drunk coffee from at that last fatal meeting still lying in the sink, as Rory had left them, full of water. I went upstairs to the Laird's study, still clutching the note I had written, perhaps hoping for a miracle that Rory would be standing by the fire waiting, smiling, holding out his arms. He would have a wonderful explanation so that we could still have our happy ending.

But the study was deserted with only dead ashes of the fire. There was the chair on which we had sat in some happier world long ago, the imprints of our heads still resting on its velvet cushion. I looked around this room I had grown to love, imagining it as it might have been, my very own, the hub of this house where I would live for the rest of my life with Rory.

Staring from the writing desk was the miniature of a girl with red-gold hair whose sad eyes had watched me in the spinney when I rescued the lamb and first met Rory. I would still see her clearly when all else on Clodha had vanished, a ghost staring through the barred windows of the turret. And for the first time, instead of being sorry for myself, I felt anger. Anger that everything wrong between Rory and me was somehow the fault of this girl, the first witch, who still had the evil power to make so many innocent people suffer from her tragedy of two hundred years ago.

'Go home ... go home ...' Rory had

said. I would do just that. But before I went I intended to have a few words with the ghost of Castle Clodha. Furiously, and quite unafraid of what I might find waiting, I ran up the spiral stairs to the turret room and flung open the door.

All was exactly as it had been when Rory brought me here that first visit to Castle Clodha. Weeks — or was it a million years — ago? The broken-down chair, the spinning-wheel, the hideous wooden mantelpiece put in by a prolific Victorian MacMhor so that extra servants could be induced to sleep in this haunted room with its curse scratched on stone by Rowan, while she and her unborn child starved to death so that the chief of MacMhor, who rescued her from Eilean na Gealach and made her his mistress, could fix his eyes and hopes on a rich mainland bride.

I shuddered in pity for poor Rowan. The room was intensely cold, as it must have been when she died, the feeling of horror remained as though her tragedy had been enacted but yesterday. Not only cold but a crawling sense of defeat and terror.

These emotions were strangely mine for a very different reason.

'You've won, Rowan!' I cried to the silent walls. 'You can add Rory to your collection. I don't care – do you hear, I don't care what happens to your wild MacMhors.' And suddenly I burst into tears and dragging off the MacMhor betrothal ring I flung it across the room at the mantelpiece. Somewhere I heard it strike wood and rattle away into silence.

I walked out of Castle Clodha proudly after that, without even a backward glance. Walking down the hill, I noticed the harbour was busy already, although it was only six in the morning. I remembered the early-morning catch taken by the fishing boats into Oban. Very well, that suited my plans. Instead of waiting hours for the ferry and risking another encounter with Rory, I would get one of the fishing boats to take me across.

As I went into the cottage, I realised I still had one other problem with no easy solution. At that moment I felt utterly unable to face Gran's bitter disappointment when I told her about

Rory and me.

Perhaps Katrine would have the answer. She was in the bedroom.

'Heard the news, May? They've found a dead man on the beach.'

'Is it – is it Felix Hall?'

Katrine put down her hairbrush and turned round. 'I think *that*'s most unlikely. Felix Hall – why should you think it was him?'

'Well, Colin thinks someone – might have killed him.'

'Colin,' she repeated and laughed. 'Colin has a wildly dramatic mind.'

I took a deep breath, forcing the words out. 'Colin thinks Rory has something to do with Felix Hall's disappearance.'

Katrine turned back to the mirror to fix her hair. 'Oh, really,' she said in tones of complete disinterest.

'Colin thinks Rory killed him.'

Our eyes met in the mirror, but instead of the horrified expression I expected to see Katrine looked distinctly amused. 'Oh, for heaven's sake, May – you don't surely take any notice of what Colin says about Rory. You *don't* think he killed Felix, do you?'

'I saw him with a gun, Katrine, the night you were in Glasgow when Felix disappeared.'

'Well, I wouldn't let that worry you. So did everyone else on Clodha see him with a gun. Rory was merely depicting an impressive but rather archaic sight of the MacMhor protecting his people, quelling an invasion of the hated English – oh, sorry, I forgot,' she added with a grin.

'Don't apologise, I'm not touchy on that subject. Protecting his people, Katrine, that is precisely what Rory said to me afterwards.'

'Did he tell you he had killed Felix?'

'No.'

'Then what are you worrying about? He always goes on like that.' She paused and looked at me cynically. 'You are an odd girl and no mistake. Fancy suspecting the man you love and are going to marry would be capable of such villainy.' She sprang up, her eyes wide. 'Good heavens, May, you aren't *serious?*' And when I didn't answer she added: 'It strikes me that you have an awful lot to learn about Rory MacMhor before you rush off to the altar with him.'

'You honestly don't think he killed Felix?'

Now for the first time she looked absolutely shocked. 'Rory? Oh, no. No.'

There was one thing more I had to know. 'Katrine, did you telephone me at the castle yesterday and ask me to meet you at the tower?'

She stared at me. 'At the tower? What on earth for?'

'Whoever it was pretended to be you and said that Rory was in danger.'

'Me? You must have had the island practical joker at work. I certainly didn't telephone you. I was away with Gran on the other side of the island and when I came back I called to ask how Rory was and he answered the phone.'

Further questions were interrupted by the front door bell. Apprehensively I followed Katrine, wondering who might be the early caller. It was Sandy, now unromantically returned to the role of Clodha postman, the magnificent piper of our Ceilidh vanished until the next celebration.

'I'm just away to take the early mail and I remembered there was a letter for Miss Lachlan. Ach, I'm very sorry, but with all the festivities and the other excitement I forgot to deliver it,' he added shamefacedly, 'and seeing it is from London, I thought it might be important. It must be grand getting news from the great capital city of England.'

'Any news from the harbour?' asked Katrine.

'Aye, there is now. Right enough it was. The poor mannie was washed overboard and drowned from the boat that capsized outside the harbour at Oban. Washed away out here. It often happens like that with the strange tides from Eilean na Gealach.'

'You're absolutely sure?' I said. 'He has been identified?'

Sandy gave me an odd look. 'Aye, by some chum of his in Oban. Colin MacMhor now, he was in a terrible state, he thought it might be the English gentleman.'

It was too much and I fled upstairs and seized my suitcase. I must get away immediately. How could I ever meet Rory again after this.

My eyes rested suddenly on Castle Clodha glowering down on us all from the top of the hill. It was still something from a fairy-tale. And as far as I was concerned, so it would remain, Castle Clodha – and Rory MacMhor – May Lachlan's fairy-tale that never could come true. And added to it all was the bitterness I would carry for the rest of my life, that losing Rory, destroying every chance of happiness between us, had been all my own doing. As I ran downstairs I breathed a final prayer that I would at least be spared the humiliation of having ever to meet him face to face again.

'May, May? Where on earth are you going now with that?' said Katrine, pointing to my suitcase.

'I must get away from Clodha. Before Rory comes back. I couldn't bear to see him again.' And I had to tell someone of my folly. Katrine's shoulder seemed as good for a cry as anyone else's. Overwrought, half-crazed with remorse, I sobbed out my wild tale.

'Sit down, sit down for goodness' sake,' said Katrine, not unkindly. 'Here, drink this,' and she pushed a cup of tea into my hands. 'Now, start from the beginning, what's it all about?'

I went over it, sipping tea, drying tears, trying to sound reasonable and articulate. At the end she nodded slowly: 'Yes, I think you're very wise to go, May. You were rather a silly girl to consider marrying Rory in the first place. After all, you were warned – remember Tanoth MacMhor's prophecy when you met her in her cottage that first time, to say nothing of the ghostly Rowan, who seems determined to lure you to your doom by lifting covers of wells and sawing through bicycle brakes.' She nodded sadly. 'It's worse for you, because she must really hate someone who isn't of the island.'

'Katrine – I want your help. What am I to do?'

She stood up, smiling gently. 'I'll help you, May. Yes, dear, I'll help you.'

'Do you know someone with a boat? I must be away before Rory returns.'

'All right. Got everything?' She looked

swiftly around the room. 'If there's anything you've forgotten I'll forward it. Let's go.'

'What about Gran?'

'The way you decided is best. Write her a letter and I'll see the news is broken to her gently. I'll explain everything, don't worry, now.'

'Promise?'

'I promise.'

She put my suitcase into her car and we went down to the now quiet harbour, the boats already moving out to sea.

'Aren't you curious about your letter?' she asked.

I was still clutching the envelope in my hand. I tore it open and a letter from Jim Scott and a cheque for £200 fell out, with his very best wishes for my future happiness.

'You were wrong about one thing, Katrine, Rory certainly wasn't interested in my money. Look . . .'

But Katrine wasn't interested. 'Thank goodness the weather is fine today,' she said, 'there will be no trouble getting across.'

'You know someone who'll take me?'

She laughed. 'I'm going to take you myself. It's easy. I've often driven Colin's motor-boat. Out you get.' For a moment she looked along the line of boats moored on the beach. 'Over there, that one of Colin's. He won't mind.'

'Are you sure?' I asked, as we pushed it out, and throwing in my suitcase I clambered aboard. 'Will it be all right, Katrine? Won't Colin mind?'

Katrine shook his head. 'I've often borrowed this one. Do stop worrying.'

Within two minutes I could see that Katrine was equally good and equally reckless in a boat as she was in a car. But at that moment I felt it was of little importance if I ever saw land or Oban or Clodha again. Clodha was growing smaller when suddenly a small figure ran down to the harbour, waving frantically.

Even at this distance it looked like Tanoth MacMhor. I felt sudden guilt that I hadn't said goodbye to her, afraid that she would be hurt and not understand my rejection of Rory. How could she understand it?

I stood up and waved back. She was motionless now, her arm upraised, the angle of the sun touching her light hair with gold.

'Sit down, May, what on earth are you doing?' said Katrine.

'I'm waving goodbye to Tanoth.'

'Tanoth?' Her head swivelled round. 'Where?'

'At the harbour – look near the end of the pier.'

Katrine narrowed her eyes. 'I can't see anyone.'

'You must. Look at her . . .'

Katrine shrugged and turned away. 'I can't see her,' she said emphatically. 'Not that I'd want to. Pity you can't take her with you. Clodha would be well rid of her *too*.'

I realised that though Tanoth was plain to me, perhaps Katrine was too vain to admit to being short-sighted. When I looked again Tanoth had gone, her departure marked with her usual speed. I was sorry still that somehow I had let her down, with her simple faiths and loyalties. I had run away indeed, in the most cowardly fashion deserting Rory, without a word of apology, deserting Gran, without telling her I was going, and now deserting Tanoth, that childlike creature so eager to be my friend, was somehow the last straw in degradation.

Too miserable and withdrawn to care much where we were going, suddenly I realised I was seeing the other side of the island, the side where only the sheep grazed, too barren, too sunless to support much life.

'Katrine, this isn't the way to Oban.' I hardly liked to mention the fact, in case it had something unknown to me to do with tides, for she was certainly steering very confidently.

'I'm putting Eilean na Gealach between us and whoever might be returning from Oban. See ...' She pointed triumphantly across the water where a glimmering streak of white, remarkably like Colin's speedboat even at this distance, raced towards Clodha, leaving silver foam in its wake.

'No need to tell you who that is. Well, you wouldn't want Rory to see us, would you?' And the motor roared into life once more.

I remembered having been on this part

of the sea once before. The afternoon spent in the speedboat with Colin and Felix Hall when they were discussing turning Clodha into a holiday camp. How keen Felix had been to drive the powerful speedboat, showing off, trying to get too close to Eilean na Gealach, not realising how dangerous the rocks thrusting like a hand out of the sea were, until the boat began to rock.

The motor-boat was rocking too. I looked round swiftly and regardless of the throbbing engine we were drifting towards the wicked-looking rocks. If we were taken into the current in this old boat, remembering how Felix and I had been tossed on to the floor of the high-powered boat, in this one we wouldn't stand a chance.

'Be careful – we're far too close.'

Then the current had us and the boat began to pitch from side to side. The engine whined and cut out. 'Katrine, for heaven's sake, watch where you're going.'

Katrine smiled and switched off the engine. Immediately we were bouncing like a cork over the waves towards the black-shining mass of Eilean na Gealach, the Isle of the Moon.

She looked at me, calm and still smiling, while outside the boat the world did a crazy dance, a waltz where sea and sky intermingled, swept apart. ... A moment later we were blinded with spray.

'It's not where I'm going, May dear. It's where *you're* going this time. And for good.'

A cold feeling of horror, of unbelief, tugged at me. 'What do you mean?' But even as I uttered the words I saw it all very clearly.

Colin's mechanic saying someone had a 'spite in' for the old bike, which almost sent me to my death on the cliff road. And Katrine's own words condemning her; blaming it on Rowan's ghost. But how did Katrine know the cover had been lifted off the sunken well when I went to the tower to meet her, and how did she know the bicycle brakes had been sawn through?

But clearer than any I saw the full glass of whisky that was mine, untouched throughout the evening at the

Ceilidh and how Rory had drunk it down and how rat poison would have killed someone not already anaesthetised by food and whisky. Like me.

Chapter Seventeen

'WHY did you try to poison Rory?' I asked, hoping to jolt her into sanity.

I thought it had the desired effect, for she turned pale. 'How was I to know he would drink your glass?' she asked sullenly and the last of my suspicions fell neatly into place.

'Do you realise what you're saying, that you're admitting you tried to poison me?'

She covered her face. 'I didn't mean to – I thought I'd make you ill, frighten you away from Clodha. Oh, why did you come here in the first place, everything was going so well until you came.'

We were shouting at each other in an endeavour to be heard. I had to keep calm, if I turned hysterical, or lost my nerve now, we would both hurtle into that roaring maelstrom Eilean na Gealach and vanish to our doom.

'Well, it's finished now. Your troubles are at an end, Katrine. No need to fear me any longer. I'm leaving of my own accord. Now for heaven's sake, while we still have time, let's try and get back to Clodha.'

I made a move forward, but she grasped my wrists and threw me back into my seat. The effort of moving almost had us capsized and for a moment we were both breathless trying to hold on to the boat. When at last it was calmed she said: 'No — we're not going back — ever. Do you really think Rory will let you go, now that he loves you? Oh, how could he ask a girl like you to marry him, and you not knowing, not understanding him at all? You still don't understand, do you? Once Rory loves someone or something *nothing*, nobody will keep him from it. If you go now, he'll be down to London within the week to bring you back to Clodha, if' — and she looked at me, her hair drenched with spray, her eyes bright, terrifying —

'if you're still alive.'

Far away a distant blur of green was Clodha. On the other side I heard the strange sound men once believed to be the siren's song, the sea moaning in Eilean na Gealach. Nearer, nearer, we drifted, holding on to the sides of the boat grimly, to keep it balanced.

'He doesn't need me any more now,' shouted Katrine above the noise of the sea, 'and once you're dead, he'll be convinced the curse of Tanoth has struck the MacMhors again. I might as well die, too!' she cried. 'I'd rather be dead right now than spend the rest of my life waiting for him, knowing that he'll never come for me.'

At least on the subject of Rory, Katrine's feelings and mine were identical. Only I still had my sanity.

Who knows, if I had waited hopefully most of my life, loving him desperately, then seeing him fall in love with a girl from London, a holidaymaker staying with her grandmother on Clodha, perhaps then I too would be like Katrine, on the brink of madness. Strange how with death only yards away I could still feel sorry for her.

'You don't know about Isobel, do you? You think that was an accident when she fell down the cliffside gathering botanical specimens.' She laughed wildly. 'That was my fault too. My fault she died. I could have saved her. She was hanging on to an old root, shouting: "Put out your hand, Katrine, please put out your hand" ...' For a moment Katrine's voice was lost above the noise of the sea and water swept into the boat on all sides, drenching us. 'But I was too scared that I would fall. I stood there watching her face as she fell.'

Katrine took her hands off the edge of the boat and covered her face. 'No, no, Isobel – I can still see her eyes as she fell. I can hear her screaming. Listen, listen ...' She looked at me wildly. 'There – don't you hear her?'

I saw my chance and took it, scrambling forward on hands and knees towards the motor. I was almost there when she turned:

'No – no – get back.'

'Katrine, let's go back to Clodha. Let's try, there's still time.'

290

She shook her head. 'Not for me. I have nothing to live for.'

'Don't be a fool, you have Colin to live for. Think of him for a change, he's loved you for years.'

'Yes, it would have been all right, but you came to Clodha and brought nothing but misery for everyone. I never was haunted by Isobel seeing her everywhere – remembering that last day – until you came.'

'Stop torturing yourself, you weren't to blame for her death. Anyone would have behaved as you did, been terrified you would both fall ...'

She looked at me wildly, her long black hair drenched with the sea, plastered against her face, her eyes bright with terror. 'You haven't any idea what it's like, being haunted as I am. And knowing it was all in vain that Rory loves another girl, when you know that you could make him happier, that he *must* love you, when you've waited so long.'

Her words were drowned by the white foam raging over the boat. She took her hands away and leaned to one side. The boat twisted, rolled: 'Goodbye, May!' she cried above the sea's thunder.

'Don't – don't ...' I screamed. Then we were both in the water. I managed to seize her shoulder, then her arm, but she threshed about, fighting me off. Suddenly the boat was on top of us and Katrine went limp.

I saw blood on her forehead as the boat danced idiotically away into the foam, a dance of death to end as smashed timber on Eilean na Gealach. My swimming, learned in the city baths, was purely rudimentary, and the struggle to keep us both afloat was a hideous timeless torture. I tried to hold Katrine up, fight against the torrent, but inch by inch I knew the battle was lost. Even if I let her go, I could never hope to swim against such a tide. Then at the end the air was full of thunder, the terrible vibration as a maelstrom took us and together we sank. ... So this was death.

And Colin MacMhor's voice came clearly. 'You keep a good grip now.'

Then Rory saying: 'If we both drown, there'll be no more quarrelling over Clodha.'

The sea was in my eyes, my lungs, its vicious weight beating me down, down ... What was the use of fighting when all hope was gone? Why didn't I die and get it over with – why should it take such a long time?

I opened my eyes and saw the blue sky above me. Perhaps this was heaven, for the strong arms that held me were Rory's, his face, his voice. 'Darling girl, it's all right. You can let go of Katrine – yes, yes, Colin has her.'

Unceremoniously I was hauled into the speedboat. Rory wrapped me into a blanket and dripping wet I was close in his arms. I saw Colin's back at the wheel and knew no more.

When next I opened my eyes there was a great canopy of brocade above my head. I put out my hand and encountered a soft white pillow. I was in the four-poster bed in Castle Clodha. Rory's bed. And a small shadow came out of the dusk, with long pale hair.

'Tanoth.' She smiled and beckoned to someone else.

I had indeed reached the end of my journey. Rory took me in his arms and held me as if never to let me go.

'Darling, heart's darling,' he whispered.

'Katrine? Where is she?'

Rory sighed. 'In Oban.'

'Is – is she—'

Rory shook his head. 'No, she isn't – richly though she deserves to be. We could hardly disentangle you both, she would be dead – drowned – had it not been for you. You saved her life by holding her afloat.' He stroked my hair back from my face, still damp and smelling of the sea. 'Katrine got a crack on the head and Colin took her to the hospital in Oban. He phoned to say she'll be all right.' He paused, his dark face anxious and afraid. 'My darling, can you ever forgive me for being so dense? I never had the slightest idea you were in any danger from Katrine. I thought you were being silly and over-imaginative.' He laughed grimly. 'Then Colin told me about the bike that had been deliberately wrecked. He hinted that he suspected Katrine might do you some harm. That was in Oban, a few hours ago – heavens, it seems like years – when we took the

294

drowned man over ...'

'Oh, Rory, I'm so ashamed. Don't talk about forgiveness after what I thought you had done. I accused you of murder, didn't I?'

Rory stroked my forehead gently. 'Hush, darling, it was my own fault. I'm too damned proud, but even I was getting scared. If anything had happened to Felix Hall, then I was certain to be suspect number one.'

'So there's still no news?' And I thought, The tide of disaster between Rory and me isn't yet at an end. There was no hope of a life for us until Felix Hall ...

But what was Rory saying? 'I couldn't believe my eyes. When Colin and I reached Oban last night with the Coastguard and the drowned man there on the quayside waiting for us was Felix Hall, large as life and twice as obnoxious, especially when he heard Colin's story that until we got a closer look everyone presumed the dead man was himself.'

'What on earth had he been up to?' I said, no longer merely relieved at Hall's reappearance but furious that this wretched man who had caused us so much misery would probably enjoy every moment of our discomfort.

'After Colin refused to let him have the speedboat to have another crack at Eilean na Gealach himself he decided he wasn't going to be beaten by a bunch of rocks. "Anyone can do anything" is his motto, so he tried to hire a boat in Oban, which he couldn't manage, as with the Convention, etcetera, there wasn't one to be had, so he tried further down the coast to buy one − with success. Idiot that he was, he nearly got himself drowned but luckily − or unluckily − as you wish to regard it, the Coastguard was patrolling near Eilean na Gealach. They picked him up unconscious with no sign of a boat anywhere. They put him in hospital with a bash on the head and when he came round he couldn't remember a thing. Until Colin reported him as a missing person and the hospitals were searched with his description. That brought him back to his senses, or whatever of that commodity he retained . . .'

After that I slept. The deep and complete sleep of one from whom the last burden is lifted. Next day, when I was on my feet, tired still but none the worse for my adventure, Rory told me about Tanoth's magic.

I said, nestling in his arms by the fire in the Laird's study, 'I feel as if a miracle had happened ...'

He stroked my hair. 'A miracle did, May. There isn't any other explanation. Remember I told you that Colin confessed he thought Katrine was up to something. Well, after that, I couldn't get back to Clodha quick enough and even Colin, pretending to be cynical and all the rest, was frightened. It was as if we both knew something was wrong. When we reached the mainland there was Tanoth standing at the pier. She looked terrified, frantic and she pointed over to Eilean na Gealach and shouted your names. We needed no second warning, we were off like a shot and almost too late at that.'

'She tried to warn me too,' I said. 'Just as the boat moved off. I saw her on the pier, waving, but Katrine pretended not to notice her — said I was imagining things, that there was no one there.'

Rory looked at me strangely. 'Katrine was right — you were imagining things.'

'Oh, how could I be ...?'

'Because, dear girl, Tanoth — the real Tanoth — was on the other side of the island, helping a crofter's wife to deliver a baby. The woman is no longer young and this was the first child. At least four people, including Sandy Lachlan, who drove her there and drove her back just half an hour after we rescued you from Eilean na Gealach, will swear to her presence ten miles from Clodha village.'

'Then who ...?'

'Rowan,' he said slowly. 'You see there was a difference ...'

'Of course, I remember, Rory. Even away in the boat the sun was gleaming on her hair, I thought — it looked red-gold.'

We were silent for a moment then I asked: 'What about Katrine?'

'Colin phoned from Oban. As I told you, she's recovering well from her head injury, but the doctors suspect she's on the verge of a complete nervous breakdown.'

I knew then I would never tell Rory how she felt responsible for Isobel's death. Let the dead bury their dead, the past was over and perhaps psychiatric miracles would happen for Katrine too.

'What will become of her?'

'Colin will wait and he'll marry her as he always intended. It's more than she deserves. When I think of her trying to lure you to the tower and lifting the grating from the well – Sandy Lachlan saw her phoning from the box at the home farm, incidentally, and he was the one who replaced the cover on the well. His watch strap had broken during the Ceilidh and he'd come back to search for it. He thought the cover had been taken off by some of the drunken revellers. It wasn't until he called two hours ago that I learned the truth: "Did Katrine tell you about the grating?" And the whole story – from his angle – came out ...'

'Please, Rory, I don't want Katrine hurt any more.'

'She won't be – not by me, unless she ever sets foot on Clodha again,' he added grimly.

'She only did it because she loved you, and for such a long time, Rory.'

He sighed. 'And fool that I was I never saw it.' He smiled at me shyly. 'You may not believe this but I never was really in love – although I was fond of Isobel and we had a great deal in common – but no girl was ever to be the moon and the stars for me until the day I saw a new face on Clodha, a foreign girl from London. She had red hair and was cooing silly baby-talk to one of my lambs. And what a temper she had.' He laughed. 'Then the very next day I saw her . . .'

' "Looking very much at home by my hearth," ' I quoted.

'Fancy you remembering what I said. Afterwards I blushed for those words, wondering if you thought it was a very corny line I was shooting. Strange,' he said, brushing my cheek with his lips, 'I knew then you were my own girl, that given half a chance I would fall in love with you. And now I know something I didn't realise before,' he continued solemnly. 'After yesterday's terrors, when I thought I had lost you, I can hardly bear to let you out of my sight. I can't risk the curse of Clodha falling on you too, I can't risk any more danger for you. May, I'd rather send you away on the next ferry and live here in Castle Clodha for the rest of my life alone than risk anything happening to you – I love you – so much . . .'

I put my arms around his neck. 'Now you listen to me, Rory MacMhor. I never was in danger from your silly legend. Only from Katrine's jealousy. That was absolutely all. And I'm not going anywhere – here I am and here I mean to stay. There's got to be something in life – in loving someone – stronger than a dead witch's curse. Love *must* be stronger, Rory, it's got to be, otherwise life isn't worth living and struggling for.'

In the few days left before our wedding, Gran became a frequent visitor, insisting she give Tanoth a hand in the kitchen 'as was right and proper as May's only relative'. Occasionally she eyed us sternly: 'I am not sure whether it is proper for the bride to be living under this roof before her wedding – in the old days now it was the done thing, but ach, it would not have been smiled upon, Rory MacMhor, in your father's day.' To me she added apologetically, 'Himself thought you should have Tanoth to look after you, he thought seeing you carried into my cottage half-drowned might give me a heart attack ...' She laughed scornfully. 'You are a silly man, right enough.'

'Maybe I am, Gran, maybe I am.' He put an arm around her and beaming, she said: 'I'm not so frail as you both think and I mean to live long enough to dandle my great-grandchildren on my knee – and knit their socks for the school.'

A few hours before our wedding I opened the door to Colin. When I heard Rory's footsteps on the spiral stairs I wondered in some alarm what would happen next.

'Well, Colin MacMhor, and what would you be wanting?' Rory demanded sharply.

'I've come to say goodbye. I couldn't resist a look at my cousin's face when he knew he was getting rid of me for ever.' Then Colin did a surprising thing, he held out his hand. 'Come, man, let's part as friends. We never did have much regard for one another, but I am not going down to England without saying I am sorry that in the past we have not been better friends.'

In the silence that followed Rory looked stern and unmoving, Colin more and more embarrassed. 'We both of us nearly had a terrible lesson in false pride, Rory MacMhor. If it hadn't been for our family ghost we would both of us have lost the girls we love . . .'

'Aye, Colin man, you're right there,' said Rory, and took his cousin's extended hand, probably the first grip in friendliness in the whole of their lives. 'How's Katrine?'

'Felix Hall knows somewhere in England where she can be completely cured of this – this nervous thing.' He turned to me. 'May, you saved her life. I know it's rather a lot to ask after what she did, but she wants you to forgive her before we leave. I know all about it, she's told me everything, but I still love her. I always will, whatever she did or tried to do,' he added defiantly. 'It's awful I

303

suppose, but it makes no difference. I cannot change the love in my heart for Katrine.'

Suddenly he shrugged in his old easy manner. 'We'll be getting married in England, once she is well again, and Felix has offered me a partnership in the firm.'

'Man, that's fine news,' said Rory with a broad smile.

'I thought you would be pleased,' said Colin, and eyeing me in his old insolent way added: 'It doesn't look as if it would be worth my while staying around hoping to be chief of MacMhor – once you marry May here. No doubt she'll give you plenty of sons.'

They both laughed and as I blushed furiously, Rory put an arm around my shoulders and said, solemnly clearing his throat: 'Hmmph, I'd greatly appreciate it, Colin MacMhor, as my closest kin, if you would do me the honour to be best man at my wedding.'

Colin grinned delightedly. 'Do I get to kiss the bride afterwards? I do. Well, what do you think I came for, anyway?'

There was new admiration born for

the MacMhors on Clodha from that day when the two cousins, long-hating rivals, entered the church side by side, in the ceremonial dress of their clan. Tanoth was my bridesmaid, for no one better deserved to walk at my side as in the years to come, her gentle sweetness stayed with us and with our children, who adored her, in their turn.

Accompanied by Sandy Lachlan, who piped us from the church we went to the harbour and watched Colin sail away to his new life. When an hour later the castle door closed behind us — for there could be no honeymoon away from Clodha, Rory explained, at this time of year — I was utterly content. I could think of no setting happier to begin my married life than exactly where I was at that moment.

I stood admiring the new plain gold ring and Rory kissed me: 'At least it's a better fit than the betrothal ring. Give it to me when I go to Oban next week and I'll get it altered.'

And then I remembered. 'Rory, I've done something terrible. The day — the day you sent me away, I rushed up to the turret room and, just to spite your old ghost, I flung the ring at the mantelpiece – come on, we must find it ...'

'Later, my love, what's the hurry?' asked Rory softly.

'Please ...'

We ran upstairs and opened the door of the turret room. Then we turned, looked into each other's eyes.

'There's something – different. Don't you feel it?' said Rory. 'About the room?'

I ran over to the fireplace. 'I think I can see the ring – behind the wood there.'

'Yes – I see it. There's no way of getting at it, except by pulling the mantelpiece away.' He touched it experimentally, gave it a sharp tug. There was a sharp crack and the whole top board, old and insecure, rotted with damp, left the wall. Behind it in the cobwebs of more than a hundred years nestled the MacMhor betrothal ring.

Rory blew the dust off it. 'Here you are.' He handed it to me. 'There's the curse of Clodha too, see it scratched on

306

the stone. Read it for yourself,' and he blew the dust away:

MacMhor betrayed and murdered me
Accursed from now MacMhor shall be . . .

I thought of the lovely girl in the miniature, her only fault that her lover was greedy for gold. I thought of her terrible slow death. 'Poor Rowan, poor Rowan.'

'That's odd,' said Rory, 'there are other words written beneath – do you see them? Look – on this other stone. Listen . . .'

''Til May a MacMhor's heart has won,
Then this dire curse shall be undone.'

'I knew there was something different about the room,' he said. 'Can't you feel it?'

'Yes – that terrible coldness. It's gone.'

And with it had gone the hostility, the sadness. Now it was only a vacant room, poor and shabby, but no longer sinister. The spell was broken and Rowan's power to destroy the MacMhors was lost for ever.

'May darling. We're free.' And Rory's laughter rang through the castle. We were free to live, to love. And so it was, until time itself passed and all other life but that of Clodha faded from our dreams.

DENISE ROBINS TITLES IN LARGE PRINT

CATHERINE DARBY TITLES IN LARGE PRINT

Falcon for a Witch

A Game of Falcons

Fortune for a Falcon

FRANCIS MURRAY TITLES IN LARGE PRINT

Castaway

The Heroines Sister

Dear Colleague

ROSALIND LAKER TITLES IN LARGE PRINT

The Smuggler's Bride

Ride the Blue Riband